Moore Field
School and the Mystery

Moore Field
School and the Mystery

Liam Moiser

Strategic Book Publishing and Rights Co.

Strategic Book Publishing and Rights Co.
12620 FM 1960, Suite A4-507
Houston TX 77065
www.sbpra.com

ISBN: 978-1-62516-787-3

Acknowledgments

I want to thank all the people who have supported me throughout the project, and I want to especially thank my mother for always believing in me.

Contents

Chapter 1

Shock for the School

It was a cold winter's day, and Samantha was walking home with one of her friends after a long, hard day at school.

"So what do you think?" asked Laura suddenly. She was a couple of years older and, unlike Samantha, was average height for her age; Samantha was really tall and very skinny. She smiled as she waited for Samantha to answer the question.

Samantha, who had been daydreaming, suddenly looked up; she had no idea what Laura was going on about.

"About?" Samantha asked.

"About the school closing," Laura replied.

The school that the children had been going to was closing at the end of the week when the term ended. The school had been going for more than one hundred years, but due to more parents sending their children to one of the public school in the city, there was no need for the small private school run by Miss Moore anymore, so she had decided to sell the school to a man who wanted the building for his firm to move into. Samantha's mother and father worked at the school and had done so for as long as she could remember. The school five years ago was thriving with more than one thousand pupils on the books and a waiting list of three hundred, but now it only had seventy pupils, which meant that it wasn't making the money to keep it going.

"Oh," giggled Samantha, "I think that it is really sad that something so old is closing down, and I really hope that Miss Moore can find something to do with all the spare time she will have."

"I do too." Laura sighed.

"I also really hope that you and I can stay together, though I doubt it. My mother and father are thinking of moving out of the city so they can find jobs teaching, hopefully, in a small village. Well, that is Dad's dream, anyway. Apparently he has always wanted to teach in a village school. He says there is more you can teach them," Samantha replied.

Laura looked at Samantha and sighed. "And my parents want me to go to Public school. They are trying to get me into one for next term. They say that with my exams just a few months away, I am going to have to stay in school and get ready. I am sure that I am going to hate it. I haven't been in public school at all; I had a tutor until I was ten, and then I came to Moore Field School."

"I am sure that you will be great. If you do go to a secondary school, I bet you will be very popular at the school," smiled Samantha, who, unlike Laura, had gone to a primary school and had liked it, though she didn't like saying goodbye to her friends when they had gone up to secondary school and she had joined the boarding school. Only Jessica had gone to Moore Field with her, and they were still good friends, though she hadn't been at the school that day due to illness. Samantha and Jessica had been friends since they had first started primary school, and Samantha missed her badly.

"I am sure Jessica will be at school tomorrow," Laura suddenly said, realising that Samantha was thinking about it. She was also friends with Jessica and missed her too.

"How did you know that was what I was thinking?" Samantha giggled.

"I had this feeling." Laura laughed. "I am sure that I will like it there. The only problem is that I can't play tennis every day."

The school that they went to encouraged the students to follow their dreams. Samantha was great at the piano, and Laura was great at tennis, and so for one hour a day, all the pupils did what they were good at. There were high hopes that, with the right training and support, both of them could be successful in what they did: The school had been responsible for no fewer than forty famous people, ranging from tennis stars to musical stars.

"I'm sure that they will have P.E. at the school. I know it won't be every day like it is at our school, but I am sure that you will still be able to practice a lot." Samantha sighed; the primary school she had gone to had only had two P.E. lessons a week.

"I hope you're right," Laura said as they turned down the street they lived on. They hadn't moved more than a few yards when Laura suddenly stopped.

Samantha looked at Laura before asking, "Why have you stopped?"

Instead of speaking, Laura pointed at her friend's house. In front of it was a blue car, which Samantha didn't find odd because it was her parents' car, though she was wondering why it was there so early. They didn't normally get home until 6:00 p.m., but then she suddenly saw what Laura was pointing at—a green car that belonged to Miss Moore; well, it had the same plate number.

"What is Miss Moore doing at your house?" Laura asked.

"I have no idea," sighed Samantha. She was sure that normally the staff did all their meeting at school.

"Well, maybe she wants to speak to your parents about how naughty you have been," Laura suggested wickedly.

"I don't think so. You are forgetting that my mother and father work at the school, and if I had been naughty, don't you think they would have been told at the school?" Samantha giggled. "Like that time me, you, and a few mates skipped class, and Miss Moore found us and said she would write to our parents. Well, she didn't write to my dad; she asked me to wait in the office and went to get him, and she told him there and then."

"I didn't know that." Laura sighed, "And I thought that I had gotten it hard when the letter came through the door. Dad was the one to go. Apparently most of our friends didn't get in trouble since they picked the letter up instead of their parents, so they had no idea what we did."

They walked down the street together, and once they got to Samantha's house, they said goodbye to each other, as Laura lived at the end of the street and Samantha lived in the middle. Samantha looked at both cars before taking a deep breath and opening the door. Unlike what she told Laura, she was a bit nervous in case she was in trouble, though she couldn't figure out what she could have done wrong.

Samantha looked around the room and suddenly saw Cook smiling at her. "Your parents are in the living room with Miss Moore. They are having a meeting, and they have told me to make you a glass of milk and some cookies for a snack because they don't know how long they will be."

"Do you know what is going on?" Samantha asked.

"Nope, I don't know," Cook replied sweetly, "and even if I did, I couldn't tell you. All I know is that you have to go upstairs and do your homework. Your father says he knows you have some."

"Okay." Samantha smiled back at Cook, whom she loved dearly. "Will you bring my milk and cookies upstairs to me?"

Cook looked at Samantha and smiled. "Of course I will."

"I am glad."

Samantha went upstairs and was soon in her bedroom. She quickly put her bag down on her bed and got out her math and English books. She decided to start with her math homework. Cook, true to her word, came in with the milk and cookies and helped Samantha with a question she was stuck on. Samantha knew that she would have to do the work correctly and neatly. Her mother was the English teacher whilst her dad was the head of science, so she knew that her mother would look through her work and make sure that it was all written neatly. If it wasn't, she would send her daughter back upstairs to redo it neatly. Because Samantha never wanted to do her homework twice, she would take a lot of care with it.

Meanwhile, downstairs Miss Moore and the Bakers were down at the table ready to start talking, biscuits and a pot of tea nearby.

"So, what is so important?" Mr. Baker asked.

"Oh, I just want to know if you will stay on with the school," Miss Moore replied with a twinkle in her eyes.

"But I thought the school was closing at the end of the term." Mr. Baker looked a bit shocked. Hadn't they sent out the letter last week saying the school was closing?

"We are closing." Miss Moore sighed. "Well, we are closing down here, but I was thinking over the weekend that it would be such a shame to see the school close, after all, and I remembered a lovely place called Lakeview where I lived when I was younger."

"I think I went there with my parents when I was younger," Mrs. Baker said. "If I'm not mistaken, there was a boarding school there at the time, but it has since closed."

"You are right, there was a boarding school there, but ten years ago, the owner died. They tried to sell the building, but they couldn't, so the school closed, which was a shame because it means that there is only one school within two hours' drive of the place." Miss Moore stopped to take a breath before continuing. "I wrote to the person who is selling it asking if it was still available, and the reply was yes. I am going up there in January to see if it needs any work, and if it is suitable, then I will buy it there and then."

"There's just one problem with this idea," Mr. Baker sighed.

"What is that?" Miss Moore asked.

"Well, how are we going to move the whole school to Lakeview? It would be hard to take everything," Mr. Baker said clearly.

"We wouldn't be taking everything with us," Miss Moore replied. "What we would do is take the trophies and things like that and get everything else from the big town a couple of hours' drive away from Lakeview. Also, apparently some of the equipment is still in the school, and before you ask if

6

it will be good enough, every month someone goes in and cleans the building from top to bottom and throws away what isn't good anymore."

"Well, it seems that Moore Field School will continue. I am glad about that. I was scared that we might have lost it, and like we have said before, it would be a shame to lose the school after all this time." Mrs. Baker was excited that the school would be continuing.

"I was hoping that you, Mrs. Baker, would stay on as the English teacher." Miss Moore then turned to Mr. Baker. "I was hoping that you would become the head of the junior section. Although we have just taken girls from the ages of ten through sixteen, from now on, we will be taking girls and boys from the ages of six through ten for the junior section and eleven through sixteen for the senior section. The juniors would have their own school building and bedrooms for the boarders. I think you would be a perfect choice for the head, as you have been the head of science for five years now and have done a great job in getting the exam results up."

Mrs. Baker looked at her husband. She doubted that her husband would move. She sighed, "I don't know. I know that Lakeview is more than one hundred miles away from here, so it would mean moving. I would love to, but I am not sure that Mr. Baker would want to move so far away. I loved the place and thought that it would be a great place to live someday. It was very peaceful."

Mr. Baker smiled. If his wife wanted to move, then he would try and make it happen. He loved his wife and would do anything for her. "Well, I am sure we can manage to move, but we would have to sell here first, which could mean living in a hotel for a few weeks."

"I don't mind." Mrs. Baker hugged her husband. "I've always wanted to go back to Lakeview; the scenery was wonderful when I was last there."

"So does that mean that I can count you in?" Miss Moore suddenly asked.

"Yeah, if we can find somewhere near enough and sell our house, then yes, you can count us in." Mr. Baker smiled. "And I would love to become the head of the junior school."

"I am glad that you are willing to give this a go. I was afraid that you were going to say no, and I would have to try and find someone as good as you to become the head. I trust you and your wife, and that is why I wanted you to be the first to know what I have decided."

"I think we should take a break and drink some of the tea that the cook brought in," Mrs. Baker suggested. "It will be getting cold."

Mr. Baker poured everyone a cup of tea and passed around the plate of biscuits, and they all settled down to drink their tea.

Meanwhile, upstairs Samantha had finished her homework and the milk and cookies that Cook had brought her. She went downstairs to the kitchen where she found Cook busy making dinner and handed the plate and glass to Cook.

"Have you finished your homework?" Cook asked when she realised that Samantha was still there.

"I have," said Samantha, "and now I'm getting bored."

"Well, I'm sure that your mother and father won't be too long. Why don't you set the table for me?" Cook smiled and looked at the clock. It was 6:50 p.m., and she wondered how much longer the Bakers would be with Miss Moore.

Back in the living room, they were just starting their discussion again.

Mr. Baker was the first to say something. "So when are you thinking of moving?"

"I was thinking that we should cut the rest of this year out, and we would start at the beginning of the next school calendar year, which is in September," Miss Moore replied.

"That sounds like the best idea." Mrs. Baker smiled.

"I also was thinking that we will have a head boy and girl, plus five prefects for the main school, whilst the juniors will have a head boy and girl, plus three prefects. That's to begin with, of course. If the school grows, then we will have to change things, but let's take this one step at a time." Miss Moore laughed. "The only time that the juniors and seniors will meet is on a Sunday when everyone can do what they want outside, and if it is raining, there will be entertainment inside."

Mr. Baker smiled as he looked at the big grandfather clock. "I think that sounds great."

Suddenly the grandfather clock struck seven.

Chapter 2

The Bakers Have Fun

Miss Moore jumped out of her seat. "Is that the time?"
"Yeah, it seems like the time has just flown by," Mrs, Baker laughed.

"Doesn't it seem like that?" Miss Moore laughed as she hurried around the room trying to collect her things. "I am sure that you will want to have your dinner, and here I am stopping you. I should have been back at the school half an hour ago. The caretaker will be wanting to get off, but I asked him to stay until I get back, which would be around half six."

"Why don't you stay for dinner, and I'll ring the caretaker and say you will be back soon." Mrs. Baker suggested. She was sure that Samantha wouldn't mind.

"No, thank you. I have to get the folder from the school, and then I have to type the letter for the children to take home with them tomorrow evening. I'll do one for Samantha to bring home," Miss Moore said.

"Oh, that reminds me, are we allowed to tell Samantha what is going on?" Mrs. Baker suddenly asked.

"You can as long as she—" Miss Moore started to speak, but Mr. Baker cut across.

"I don't think we should. You know she would just tell Laura and Jessica, and soon the whole school would know."

"I think you might be right." Miss Moore laughed. "That reminds me, Jessica will be back at school tomorrow. I am sure that Samantha will be happy to hear that."

"I am sure she will too," Mrs Baker said happily. "Well, since you aren't staying for dinner, I will go and call Samantha downstairs so that she can say goodbye to you. I am sure that she knows you are here."

Mrs. Baker left the room and went to the stairway. She shouted upstairs to her daughter and was startled when someone tapped her on the back.

"Yes, mother?" Samantha asked.

Mrs. Baker quickly looked around. "You scared me." She sighed. "I thought that you were upstairs doing your homework."

"I was at first, but after I finished, I realised that Cook would want the dishes from my snack to wash up," Samantha said truthfully, "then I thought that maybe she would want some help setting the table and so on whilst you and father were entertaining Miss Moore."

"Well, why don't you come and say goodbye to her?" Mrs. Baker looked at her daughter and sighed. How did someone so small mess up her hair so much? She quickly found a brush and combed her daughter's hair, and when she was satisfied that it was good enough, they went to where Miss Moore was waiting.

Samantha smiled as she looked at Miss Moore, then said in her lovely golden voice, "How do you do, Miss Moore?"

"I am fine, thank you, Samantha." Miss Moore smiled as she realised that Samantha was starting to act grown up. She was sure that one day Samantha would become something that the school and the world would be proud of. She decided there and then that she would help Samantha as much as she could, and to help her follow her dreams. She knew that Samantha was quite keen on the piano and, having heard her play, Miss Moore was sure that she could become successful. "Well, I really must be going."

"Bye, Miss Moore." Samantha said, smiling.

"Bye," Mr. and Mrs. Baker said together.

Miss Moore left the room followed by Mr. Baker, who waited at the door until Miss Moore was safely in her car before closing the door. He went back to the living room where he found his wife and daughter talking.

"So, what do you both want to do whilst we wait for dinner?" he asked.

"Oh, that reminds me, Cook said that dinner would be ready at 7:30, so that gives us, like, twenty-five minutes," Samantha said suddenly. "Can we play a game of Go Fish?" She was glad that her father wanted to play a game with her. Having a mother as an English teacher and a father as the head of science was sometimes fun, but other times it was not. Normally her father had dinner, then got on with his important paperwork whilst her mother checked her homework, then sent her to play in her room until bedtime so that she could get on with her paperwork.

"That sounds like a great idea," Mr. Baker said as he got a pack of cards off the table.

They all sat down, started to play the game, and were having loads of fun until Cook came in and told them that dinner was served.

"I think that we should leave this until after dinner," Mrs Baker suggested. "Then we can finish the game off, that's if you want, Samantha."

Samantha smiled; it had been forever since she had done anything with her mother and father. "So does that mean that you and Father don't have any work to do tonight?"

"I don't have too much, and I am sure that it can wait until after you are in bed. It seems ages since we have done something as a family." Mrs. Baker smiled.

Mr. Baker looked at his wife and daughter and said, "Well, you two can stay and chat in here if you want. I'm going to go and get my dinner before it gets too cold."

They all made their way into the dining room and were shocked to see that Cook had already put the food on the table. Normally she waited until they were all in the room before serving. They also were surprised to see that Cook had lit some candles, which made the room feel all friendly. Samantha loved how the candles flickered in the darkness, as Cook had also turned off the lights. They all sat down, and Samantha was wondering why they didn't have meals like this every day.

"This looks wonderful," Samantha said as she started to eat her roast potatoes and chicken. "I love how Cook can make food too tempting not to eat."

"I am glad she does." Mrs. Baker giggled.

"Well, why don't you eat it, Samantha, instead of talking?" Mr Baker laughed, then settled down to eat his own food.

Ten minutes later, the plates were empty and Cook took them into the kitchen to be washed up. She came back a few minutes later carrying the dessert.

Samantha looked at the dessert as Cook put a dish in front of her and smiled. It was her favourite pudding. "I love apple pie and custard."

"I know you do." Cook smiled. "Why do you think I made it?"

"I think that you are the kindest person in the world," Samantha replied.

"What about us?" Her mother and father said at the same time. "I thought that we were the kindest people in the world."

"Okay, you *all* are the kindest people in the world." Samantha giggled. She knew that she couldn't win if she just said one of them was the kindest person, and she really didn't know who was the kindest out of the three of them.

"I think that you just gave the best answer." Mr. Baker smiled at his daughter. "Now, seeing as it's your favourite food, don't you think we should eat it before it gets cold?"

"I do." Samantha smiled. She didn't like cold apple pie and custard.

They all settled down to eat their apple pie and custard, and before long, it was gone. Samantha wanted some more, but Cook said that there wasn't any, so she just had to be satisfied with what she had gotten.

"Before we go and continue our game of cards and I forget," Mr. Baker said to Mrs. Baker, "I was talking to the music teacher today, and he tells me that Samantha has really improved with her piano playing this term. He said that you and I should listen to her when we get a chance, and I was thinking we should do it tonight."

"Oh, Dad, I'm not that good yet." Samantha giggled. "I still need to improve a lot. I can't believe he said you should listen to me playing."

"Well, he says that you are one of his best pupils and that with the right help you could go far." He smiled. "So I think that we should listen to what we are missing out on."

"I agree." Mrs. Baker smiled at her daughter.

"Okay, since you are both insisting, I'll go and get my musical sheets whilst you settle yourselves down in the living room." Samantha smiled; she really did want her father and mother to listen to her music.

"Thank you," Mr. Baker said as he looked at his daughter. "We'll be waiting for you."

Samantha ran as quickly as she could to her bedroom and found her favourite piece of music, while her parents were getting settled in the living room. They couldn't wait to hear Samantha play the piano, and they didn't have to wait long. Samantha quickly cleaned her hands so that nothing could get on the piano, then rushed downstairs. She opened the door, walked to the piano, sat on the stool, and turned to see if her parents were ready.

"Are you sitting comfy?" she asked.

"We are," they replied.

"Okay," Samantha replied.

"When you are ready, you may start." Mr. Baker smiled.

Samantha turned around to face the piano, took a quick breath, and then she began to play. Mr. and Mrs. Baker were amazed at how well their daughter could play. They knew that she was good at it, but she seemed to have been practicing so hard. They smiled as she continued to play the piano, and now they knew what the music teacher meant when he had said that, with the right help, she could go far.

Samantha was enjoying herself but she was wondering what her mother and father thought. She came to the end of the piece, stopped, and turned around. "I've finished. So what did you think?"

"I think you played the piano like a pro." Mr. Baker looked at his daughter. "I think that you could become a piano player if you carry on like you are doing."

They both clapped as their daughter got up.

"I think it's time to finish off the game of cards," Mrs. Baker suggested.

"Before we do, are you allowed to tell me what Miss Moore wanted with you two?" Samantha asked suddenly, hoping to catch them out.

"I am sorry, Samantha, but we aren't allowed to tell you." Mr. Baker laughed. He had been waiting for his daughter to ask them since Miss Moore had left.

"All I can say is it is some good news," Mrs. Baker said. "Which reminds me, Jessica will be back at school tomorrow."

"That is good. I can't wait to see her." Samantha started to dance around the room.

"Okay, so it seems Samantha doesn't want to finish the game of cards off," Mr. Baker said.

"Of course I want to finish the game off," Samantha said as she quickly sat down, "You just want to end it whilst you are winning."

"You got me there." He laughed.

They continued the game of cards, which went back and forth between them all until finally Mr. Baker was the winner.

Mrs. Baker was about to speak when she looked at the clock. It was 9:30 p.m., and she knew that Samantha had school tomorrow.

"Okay, Samantha, it's bedtime." She smiled.

"Okay, mother," sighed Samantha. She wanted to argue but knew better. She hugged her father good night, then she followed her mother upstairs, and they stopped just outside of her room.

"I'll see you tomorrow," Mrs Baker said as she hugged her daughter.

"I love you," Samantha replied as she hugged her mother back.

Samantha went into her room, changed, then went straight to bed. Half an hour later, her mother came in and was surprised to see that her daughter was already fast asleep.

Chapter 3

The School Is Told

The classrooms were quiet and the school playground was deserted. To anyone going past, the school would have looked empty, but it wasn't. You see, it was quiet because the whole school was in the Great Hall waiting for Miss Moore to arrive to start this big, important assembly that they were about to have. They knew it was important because they had all been allowed to miss their last lesson completely, and quite a few of the children were feeling smug about it, whilst some of the older ones couldn't believe it.

"Do you know anything about this, Samantha?" Laura suddenly asked. She remembered that when they had walked home together, they had seen Miss Moore's car outside Samantha's house. "I am sure that she was in your house."

"She was," Samantha giggled, "though I have no idea what they were talking about." She suddenly realised that most of the people near her were looking at her. In case she had any news, they all were wondering what it was.

"Well, it just seems strange that she was at your house last night, and now she and your mother and father are the only three who are not here." Laura laughed. "Well, all I know is that it has to be something important. Are you sure that you don't know?"

"Okay, I'll tell you what I do know," Samantha said suddenly. She then realised that the whole school had gone quiet. Well, maybe not the whole school, but the rows in front of and behind her had gone quiet. "All I know is that it is some good news for the school," she said with a twinkle in her eyes. She was sure that they were expecting to be told something much bigger.

"What?" Laura looked at Samantha. "I thought you were going to tell us all something big then. You're such a tease sometimes."

"Well, you wouldn't listen to me when I said that I didn't know anything about it," replied Samantha truthfully. "Maybe next time you'll believe me when I say I don't know anything, because if I knew anything, you know I would have told you already."

"Okay, so maybe I did push you just a little bit." Laura giggled. "So do you know what your parents are doing when the school closes at the end of the week?"

"All I know is that as soon as we can, we will be leaving the city," sighed Samantha, "since my father wants to move to the countryside. He used to live in the countryside when he was a child, and apparently he loved it there, so he wants to live in another village and teach."

"Well, we are staying in the city. My parents have signed me up for a public school. They told me last night," she said sadly. "I am sure that I will hate it so much. I loved being a boarder here."

The only reason that the school didn't have any boarders was because they had decided that, as they were closing at the end of term, it would be better for everyone to be day pupils, so they had all been going home at 4:00 p.m. since September.

"I miss being a boarder, too," Samantha sighed.

"You two had better quiet down." Jessica smiled. She was glad to be back at school after her illness. She had been listening to her friends, but then she saw Miss Lawn looking at them. "Miss Lawn keeps looking at you." Jessica was seated in the row in front of Laura and Samantha. "I wonder where Miss Moore is. We have been waiting for nearly ten minutes; it's unlike her to keep everyone waiting, and I'm getting bored."

"Well, she is probably talking with my mother and father because they aren't here either." Samantha giggled. "Though I do wish that they would hurry up."

"I wish so, too," Jessica said before adding, "I hate sitting still."

"Jessica, face the front." Miss Lawn's voice suddenly filled the air; she had been keeping an eye on them for a while. "Or do you want to come and sit with me and Mr. Kingly?"

"I told you she was watching." Jessica sighed; she really wanted to talk to Laura and Samantha, but she didn't want to sit on her own with the teacher. She turned around because she knew that Miss Moore would want to know why she had been sent to the front.

"I am starting to—" started Laura as she watched Jessica turn to face the front, but that wasn't the reason she stopped. The reason she had stopped was that Mr. and Mrs. Baker and Miss Moore were walking into the hall. The whole school quickly got up, then waited for Miss Moore to get to the head's chair and give permission for them to sit down.

"I bet you are all wondering why I have asked you all to be here instead of going to your final lesson. Well, there is a good reason. As you know, the school is closing down at the end of the week." She smiled before continuing. "That was the original idea, but I was thinking a couple of weeks ago that it would be a shame to lose the school after all this time, so instead, we will be moving to Lakeview."

The school was excited, and the whole hall started to buzz with excitement, though a few wanted to know if they could go even if they stayed in Manchester.

Miss Moore seemed to read everyone's mind when she continued her speech. "We will be running a bus from here to Lakeview at the start of the school year in September, though if you decide to do this, be warned that you won't be able to come home at Christmas and Easter unless your parents come and pick you up. The bus will only go back to Manchester in July at the end of the school year." She waited for that to sink in. She was about to continue when—

"So we can stay at the school!" Jessica shouted out, she was so happy.

"Yes," replied Miss Moore, "but can you please not interrupt me? If anyone wants to ask a question, she can do it at the end of my speech."

"I promise, Miss Moore." Jessica blushed.

"Now, where was I?" Miss Moore had to think for a few moments before she could continue. "Oh, yes, that's right . . . Now as you are aware, this has been an all-girls school since we started, but we have decided that, when we start at Lakeview, we will become a mixed boarding school. In addition, we will split into two houses: junior and senior. Scholars from the ages of six through ten will be in the junior section and ages eleven through sixteen in the senior section. I didn't make the decision lightly. The reason we decided that was to increase the school population."

There were quite a lot of gasps around the room, and Miss Moore decided to allow things to settle down.

"As I was saying, school starts in September, but the week before, there will be a camp to allow students to mix. The juniors will be going to a camp with Mr. Baker, who has said that he will come with the school and become the head of the junior school."

"So that's why she was at your house last night," Laura whispered to Samantha.

"It must have been," Samantha replied.

"The seniors will be going to their own camp with me, as both senior school head and school headmistress. The only time I will ever interfere with the junior school is if Mr. Baker needs assistance.

"As I was saying before, there will be a bus in September at the start of the school year. We also will run a bus to bring students to camp. Those students will have to stay at school on the Sunday after camp ends, unless your parents pick you up, because school will begin the next day."

"That sounds . . ." started Samantha, then stopped and blushed.

Miss Moore ignored the slip from the excited girl. "Well, I think that just about sums it up." She smiled.

She was about to dismiss the students when Mr. Baker went up and whispered something in her ear. She looked at the school again as Mr. Baker went back to his seat.

"I almost forgot, a few things I have about next year. The seniors will have two houses, red and blue, and the house that does the best academically will win the house cup, this means that you will have to work together and help each other. If you see a fellow house mate struggling with homework, I want you to help them understand. Though, if anyone is caught doing the homework, for the other students in the house, then there will be a punishment. Whereas the juniors will have a red team and a blue team and will earn certificates, and the person who has the most will win a trophy." She looked around the room. There were only a few girls who were younger than ten; normally she took ten to sixteen year olds, but this term she had taken a few of the older girls' sisters as day pupils. "There also will be a head boy and head girl for the senior school; the junior school will have a head of each team, and the head could be a boy or a girl." She stopped again and smiled. "Now, that is all. Are there any questions?"

"What will happen to all the trophies in the trophy room?" asked Amy, who was at the front of the hall.

"Now, that is a great question." Miss Moore smiled. "We will take them with us, but we will be putting them in a trophy case that says Manchester Moore Field School, so everyone will know they are from the old school."

"I really like that idea." Samantha smiled happily.

"I do too," agreed Laura, whilst the rest of the school nodded in agreement.

"Well, I am glad that you like the idea, but I really think that we should get on, seeing as it is 3:50, and I am sure you will want to leave at four. I think we should get on with the questions."

The whole of the hall was buzzing as people asked Miss Moore questions and she answered them all as truthfully and as quickly as she could. After ten minutes, Miss Moore looked at the clock.

"I am sorry, children," she said as the children put their hands down, "but we will have to leave it there." She looked at her staff, who had gone over to the door. "As you can see, the teachers will be handing out a letter for you to take home. If you are going to stay, we need the letter back by Friday, because as soon as the New Year comes, I'll have left Manchester and will be living in Lakeview."

The children looked at the headmistress and smiled. They were glad that the school wasn't closing down, even if some of them couldn't continue, with it moving so far away.

"School dismissed." Miss Moore's voice suddenly filled the hallway.

The school got up and left, everyone taking a letter, even Samantha, who found the fact that her father gave her one a bit odd.

Laura looked at Jessica and Samantha before saying, "I wish I had known sooner, but like I said, my parents have signed me up for public school."

"Oh, I wish you could come, too," sighed Samantha. "Are you going to see if you can?"

"I'll try my best." Jessica smiled. "I am sure my parents wouldn't mind."

"It's more than one hundred miles away from here," said Laura suddenly. "It means that I won't get to see you much—well, I won't get to see you, Samantha, at all since your parents are trying to move to Lakeview."

As it turned out, Jessica's parents didn't mind her going and, like Samantha's, filled her letter in the night she had gotten it so she could take it in the next day. Twenty-five seniors and five of their juniors sisters signed up for camp, and Miss Moore was hoping to advertise the school in a local Lakeview paper.

The rest of the week passed quietly except for a few small incidents: Laura spilled a pot of paint and ruined her own and another student's work, and Jessica and Samantha were caught talking in an English lesson and had to stay behind.

Soon it was time for the party that happened at the end of each Christmas term. The Great Hall had been transformed with decorations, and there was a "Merry Christmas" sign at the entrance to the hall, with a big Christmas tree with loads of decorations and an angel on the top of it.

The children thought the hall looked wonderful. They couldn't wait to begin the games and have fun with their mates, as they would probably never see some of them again. They all sat down to play the first game, and soon the party was in full swing and they were all enjoying themselves. All too soon it was time for the party to end, and they had to say goodbye to each other.

Laura, Jessica, and Samantha looked at each other and sighed.

"Promise you will stay in touch." Laura looked at the other two.

"We'll try," they both promised.

"I'll miss you so much," Laura said, tears coming.

"We'll miss you, too." Jessica and Samantha were also crying.

They left the room and walked home together in silence. No one knew what to say, so they didn't say anything. They just hoped that they would keep in touch now that they were going to different schools.

Chapter 4

A Great Surprise

It was a few months after the school had closed and Samantha was being taught at home. As Jessica lived not far away, Samantha had asked if she could share the lessons. Samantha and Jessica had just finished their last lesson for the day with Samantha's mother when Samantha looked at her watch and realised that it was already 3:30 p.m., the time Laura finished school. They knew they had to hurry; otherwise, they were sure that Laura would think they were already forgetting about her, and they didn't want her to think that.

"Come on, we'd best run, or else we'll be in trouble," Jessica said.

Samantha laughed. "I'm sure that Laura will wait, but if you insist on running, I'll race and beat you."

"In your dreams." Jessica giggled and, without another word, started to run, ignoring Samantha's cries of protests.

***

They couldn't wait to get over to see Laura. They had missed her and hated that she wouldn't be joining them at Lakeview.

At least they could stay in touch, unlike what they would do with some of the people who had made arrangement to go to other schools. They were sad that she wouldn't be continuing at Moore Field School, but Laura's parents had already put her into Milton High School when they had heard that Moore Field was closing. Laura knew that come July, she would have to rely on sending Samantha and Jessica letters, which—as she kept complaining—wouldn't be the same thing.

***

They made it just as Laura was leaving school. Samantha was glad that she didn't go there—the school building looked really old, there was an awful smell coming from somewhere, and there were boarded-up windows from where people had smashed them. Most of the time, Laura had said, lessons were never finished because the students took over. She hated it, and she wasn't allowed to play tennis that much, only when her class was doing it, and she always complained about it. The frown that had been on Laura's face disappeared as she walked over to Jessica and Samantha.

"Made any friends yet?" Jessica suddenly asked. She hadn't seen Laura talk to anyone.

"A few but none as nice as you and Samantha." Laura smiled. "Why can't you ask your parents if you can come here, Jessica? I'm sure Samantha wouldn't mind."

"My mum went to Moore Field, my gran went to Moore Field, and I'll continue there." Jessica smiled. "Well, that is what Mother said a few nights ago when Father asked why I wasn't going to another school. He says that having lessons with the Bakers isn't the same as being at school."

"Come on, you two. We can chat later. I don't have to be in until five, so we can go for a small walk before we head home. Jessica is having tea at our house since her parents are bus—" Samantha stopped when suddenly she heard someone talking.

Two men were leaving the school: one very old, with grey hair, a walking stick, and a pipe, and the one young, of average height and weight, with blue eyes, black hair, glasses. He looked like he was teaching there. "Do you know that I have been at this school since just after Christmas? There is nothing. Are you sure that we should be looking here?"

"I am sure. This is the only school that begins with the letter M in Manchester, so it must be here. Remember that we are looking for a trophy from around fifty years ago." The older man sighed as he walked past the girls. He went for a light for his pipe and didn't realise in doing so that he dropped a piece of paper. As soon as they had gone, Samantha picked it up and read it.

***

School Wins Quiz Challenge

A Manchester school was celebrating last night after winning the School Quiz Championship. Headmistress Annabel Moore couldn't hide her delight after her team that included her daughter won the trophy. The school, which has only won the School Quiz Championship once before, was over the moon at their latest success. The school, M

***

And that was where the article was torn. Samantha couldn't believe that this old man would be interested in any school, and as Laura had only started the school when the younger man had, she wouldn't know anything more than what this paper said.

"Laura, will you keep an eye on this man?" Samantha suddenly asked.

"I'll do my best. I am sure they aren't from around here, or they would have heard about Moore Field closing." Laura looked thoughtful for a few seconds before speaking. "I didn't know Miss Moore had entered the School Quiz Championship. I don't recall ever seeing the trophies at the school. I wonder if the competition is still going."

"If it is, I'm going to beg Miss Moore to let us enter it. Tomorrow isn't Miss Moore coming to speak to your parents, Samantha?" Jessica smiled.

"Yeah, she is, before she goes to Lakeview to see this building where the school is going to be housed." Samantha smiled. "And my parents have already told me I'll be boarded at the school. Because Dad is going to be the head of the junior section, he'll be staying on site, and Mother is going to be busy when she isn't at school. She thinks I will make more friends if I become a boarder. Come on, let's get out of here before people think we're up to no good."

"I agree." Jessica laughed as she ran past Samantha. "Race you."

All three girls laughed as they ran off, and they didn't notice the men as they ran past them and so they didn't hear that the older man had been on the phone. He was told about Moore Field School and the fact that it closed down. The men both knew that they would have to find out more about the school.

"My contact says that the new girl, Laura, went to Moore Field. Try to find out more information from her."

"I will do my best," the other man replied. He was going to find out about Moore Field School even if it meant pretending to be Laura's friend, even though he didn't like teaching, and when they had the information they needed, they would be rich and he could give up teaching for good.

The next day, Miss Moore never turned up at Samantha's house. She had gotten a phone call to view the building earlier, as the owner wanted the deal done quickly. Samantha wondered why Miss Moore would want a place that the owner wanted to get rid of so quickly. Samantha had been present when her father had taken the phone call and had been told to say nothing to Jessica and Laura. He also told her that she probably wouldn't see them for a while because they had to get everything ready for the move to Lakeview. What was worse for Samantha was her parents refused to show her pictures of the new house, which made Samantha think it was a place that they knew she wouldn't like.

Chapter 5

Off to Camp

It had been quite a while since the Christmas party and the closing of Moore Field School in Manchester. Miss Moore had come to the new school in Lakeview in February and had been impressed with what she had seen. She decided that she would buy it there and then. In April, the paperwork had gone through, and Miss Moore sent additional camp and school information to existing students and advertised in the local paper. In the end, seventy pupils for the senior school and forty pupils for the junior school enrolled, and forty-five seniors and thirty juniors would be going to camp. She was sure that the people who had gone to the Manchester branch would be glad that the school was staying in existence.

It was finally the day of camp. Samantha and her father were going to the camp—Samantha to the senior camp and her father to the junior camp to be in charge of it. Mrs. Baker wasn't going with them; they had decided it would be best if she unpacked in their new home with Cook whilst they would have peace and quiet with no Samantha around. They had been staying in a hotel near Lakeview for the last few days. Samantha had hated saying goodbye to Laura, but since she had started school in January, they had seen each other only at the weekends. Samantha was happy when the day finally came for her and her father to go to camp because she couldn't wait to see Jessica again.

"Are you ready?" Mr. Baker asked Samantha. "We don't want to be late for camp."

"I'm ready," Samantha replied as she closed her suitcase and put it with her father's. She was just about to open the door when her mother came in.

"Don't I get a hug?" Mrs. Baker asked her daughter. She held out her hand to her daughter.

Samantha smiled as she ran to her mother and hugged her. "When will I get to see the house?" she suddenly asked.

"You will see it when you get back." Mrs. Baker smiled at her daughter, even though she knew she would see it before, seeing as the house was opposite from the senior camp. They had bought the house because it was big and in a rural area, and Mr. Baker loved the peace and quiet of rural life.

"We really should get going," Mr. Baker said. "We wouldn't want to have to walk to camp, would we?"

Samantha giggled. "No, we wouldn't. I don't think I could manage that; well, even if I could, I am sure that I would be very tired by the time we got there."

"I agree." He laughed.

Samantha went to the door and opened it before saying, "I'm ready."

"Good," said Mr. Baker as he picked up his and Samantha's suitcases.

They said goodbye to Mrs. Baker and left the hotel room. Samantha was glad that they wouldn't be staying in a hotel room after camp; it had been okay at first, but after a while, it got boring. They went to the car, and as it was only going to be Samantha and Mr. Baker, she was allowed to sit in the front. She sat with her seatbelt on, waiting for her father, who was busy putting the suitcases in the car.

Soon he got into the car, started it, looked at his daughter, and smiled. "Well, isn't this exciting."

"It is," replied Samantha.

It would take thirty minutes to get to the school, and they were excited because they hadn't seen the school building for real, just in the pictures Miss Moore had sent with her last letter. The school in the photo had looked good and big, and Samantha hoped it was big because she thought it would be more fun.

***

Meanwhile, Mrs. Baker left the hotel room and paid the bill. She had put her things and the rest of Samantha's and Mr. Baker's in the car. Most of their belongings had gone straight to their new house for Mrs. Baker to sort out. When Mr. Baker had come up to see the house a few months ago, he had bought new beds that had been set up. Cook and the maid had gone with Mr. Baker and stayed there to sort out the kitchen and clean the house so that all Mrs. Baker had to do was put everything away.

***

Samantha and her father were having fun in the car. She was seeing things other than big houses and factories. Although most of the houses were big, some of them were small with thatched roofs, called cottages, and the only factory she saw—if you could class it as a factory—was a sugar mill. (She decided that, if her father would let her, she would visit it, because she wanted to know how sugar was made.) She was enjoying seeing things that weren't in Manchester, and all too soon they were at the school.

"Wow," said Samantha with a smile, as they turned into the school car park.

They were twenty minutes early for the bus. The school already had a caretaker who was going to keep an eye on the car park for that week; he had his own building from which he could monitor the cameras all around the school. Other than the caretaker's building, there were two big buildings, one with a sign on the top reading "Moore Field Junior School" and the other, larger building's sign reading "Moore Field Senior School." Miss Moore came up to them with a big smile on her face and shook their hands. She then pointed out Jessica to Samantha, and waited for the girl to leave before asking, "So, what do you think?"

"I think that this building is great, and I am sure we will make it a success," replied Mr. Baker.

Miss Moore looked at him for a moment before continuing. "Are you sure you can handle the juniors?" She had wanted to take them all to the same camp, but Mr. Baker had suggested the juniors have cabins; he wasn't sure if they would like sleeping in tents. Miss Moore had agreed, but lately she had been having second thoughts. "You do know that it's just a twenty-minute walk to our camp if you ever need anything."

"I am sure." Mr. Baker smiled. He was really looking forward to meeting the youngsters; he loved teaching younger children and thought that there was more satisfaction in teaching them.

"I'll introduce you to the rest of the junior school staff." Miss Moore set off, then turned to see if Mr. Baker was following. It didn't take too long to find the people they had been searching for. She went up to the staff and smiled. "This is Mr Baker." She introduced the rest of the staff to him, pointing to them as she said their names. "This is Miss Smith, Mr. Brown, Miss Banks, and Miss Lionheart."

They all smiled as they said how do you do and shook hands; then, they got to know one another whilst they waited for the bus and, of course, kept an eye on the juniors.

Samantha hadn't paid attention when Miss Moore had told her where Jessica was, so she had been looking for her since she had left her father to speak privately with Miss Moore. She had passed Jessica twice, though she hadn't realised it, and was beginning to think that maybe Jessica wasn't actually there—but why would Miss Moore lie? She seemed to have been going around in a circle until she finally found Jessica talking to a boy. Samantha walked toward her.

Jessica was talking to a boy from Lakeview, hearing about what there was in Lakeview to do, but when she saw Samantha walking up to her, she ran to hug her. The boy sensed that they wouldn't want to be disturbed, so he was about to leave, but Jessica wasn't going to leave him out.

"This is Tom," she said to Samantha as she pointed to him. "He's coming to camp with us, and he is from around here."

Samantha smiled. Like Jessica, she didn't like leaving anybody out, so she went up to him with her hand held out for him to shake. "Hello, Tom. I'm Samantha."

"Hello, Samantha, it's nice to meet you." Tom smiled as they shook hands. "What do you think of Lakeview so far?"

"I think that it's good," she said.

Jessica noticed that the busses were there. It meant that they could finally get ready to set off for camp. "The busses are here!" she shouted.

Samantha, Tom, and Jessica ran up to the teachers. Going with the seniors were Miss Moore, Miss Show, Mr. Biggs, and Mrs. Knight. They were going in one bus to Camp Casper, whilst the juniors were going in their own bus to Camp Smiley. They all stood around Miss Moore, waiting for her to talk.

"I hope that everyone will enjoy him- or herself at camp and that you will all get to know one another. I also hope that everyone will behave themselves, as you will be representing the school." She looked at them all before continuing. "If we misbehave, then I am sure that the camp owner will probably not want us to go there again, and with us being new to the area, we must show them how good we all can be."

"We promise we will be good," Jessica said.

"We promise." Samantha was sure that, like her, everyone else would want to go on trips like this again. She remembered when some children had misbehaved on their trip; Miss Moore had stopped them going on any more for the rest of the year.

Miss Moore smiled at Jessica and Samantha before continuing with what she was saying. "I think I should tell you about the camps. The camp that the juniors are going to, Camp Smiley, has sleeping cabins, a dining room cabin, and an activity cabin." She looked at the juniors, who seemed to be excited. Most of them had been afraid that they would have to sleep in tents. "Mr. Baker will tell you which of the two cabins you will be sleeping in. Each day, one of the cabins will cook for the other, so you will get to learn how to cook." She stopped there and took a deep breath before turning to the seniors. "Now, as for the seniors, you will be going to Camp Casper. You will be sleeping in tents and using a campfire to cook your meals. I am sure that you will all enjoy the experience.

"The camps are at opposite ends of the same lake, so we might bump into each other. Now I think we should get on the busses."

They all climbed on to the busses. The juniors were the first to set off because there weren't as many bags for the driver to put on board, and when they did set off, they waved to the older students, whose driver took ten minutes to be off.

They sang songs to pass the time, and the teachers—except for Mr Biggs, who wasn't that keen on the noise, and so he settled down to read his book—got involved. It took them more than one hour to get to the camp, and when they did get there, they all gasped at the beautiful scenery. They all waited whilst the bus driver stopped the bus before they got out.

"Wow, this is amazing," said Samantha as she got off the bus.

"I agree," said Tom and Jessica together.

The campsite looked stunning: The lake was crystal clear, and the whole campsite was surrounded by trees. From where the seniors were going to camp, they could see two wooden cabins in the distance, which they assumed would be where the juniors were staying.

"I think I'm going to like it here." Jessica smiled.

They all agreed with her. For the rest of the day, nothing much happened except for another student, Trish, fell into the lake whilst washing the dishes that they had been using to take their tea, though no one could see how she could fall in. When it was bedtime, they were assigned to a two-person tent. Jessica and Samantha would be in one together, whilst their new friend Tom shared a tent with a boy called Ben.

Chapter 6

Having a Fun Time

Samantha was the first to awaken. She had been slowly waking for a while and looked at her watch and sighed. She knew that no one else would be up so early, and she really didn't like reading. She loved talking to people instead of sitting around bored whilst reading a book, though if there was no other choice she would, of course, read a book. She looked around the tent as she got out of her sleeping bag, then looked at Jessica, who seemed to be asleep. She wondered if Jessica would be cross if she woke her up; she decided that the risk was worth it, grabbed a pillow, and hit Jessica with it.

Jessica awoke suddenly as the pillow hit her head. She looked around the room to see what had hit her and saw Samantha giggling and holding the pillow. She was wondering what Samantha was finding funny when she asked, "What was that for?"

"I was bored," giggled Samantha, "and it looked kind of fun."

"Well, let's see if you find this fun," Jessica said as she grabbed her pillow and chucked it at Samantha, "and next time, can you please wake me up without hitting me across the head with a pillow?"

Samantha, who had seen what Jessica was planning on doing, moved out of the way, and so the pillow missed her. She quickly grabbed the pillow and said, "Now I have two pillows, and you have none. Thanks for yours. And I'll try to wake you up without hitting you with a pillow next time."

"Hey, give me that back," shouted Jessica as she got out of her sleeping bag. "I'll need that later on in case you try to hit me again."

"Well, you should have thought about that before you decided to throw it at me." Samantha giggled as she put her pillow back on her bed.

"Come on, please give me my pillow back," begged Jessica. "I promise I won't chuck it at you again, but you know I do need it."

Samantha looked at Jessica and giggled as she chucked the pillow back to her. Jessica caught it and then put it with her sleeping bag.

"What's the weather like?" Jessica asked.

"Well, if it was raining, I don't think I would still be in here." Samantha giggled. "I would have joined my dad and the juniors in their cabins so I wouldn't get wet. I'm sure that these tents can't keep the rain out, so if it does rain, I'll be the first to run."

Jessica laughed at what Samantha said. "You haven't been camping before, have you?"

"No, I haven't," replied Samantha. "How could you tell?"

"It was easy, really. Everyone who has been camping would know that tents are waterproof, except if you put things on the outside of the tent, the water can come in. If you do that, then really it's your own fault that the water came into your tent," Jessica, who had been camping loads of times, told Samantha.

"How do you know if the tent you have brought is waterproof?" Samantha asked. She still had her doubts that the tents could be waterproof.

"Well, it's easy. If the tent starts to fill with water, then it's not waterproof so that—" started Jessica but Samantha suddenly cut across her.

"So, is that the only way to tell? See, that's why I think tents are no good. I wouldn't mind camping as long as I could sleep in a cabin like the juniors are doing."

"Well, if you did that, then you wouldn't be getting the full camping experience." Jessica smiled. "Oh, and when I said you just see if the rain would come in, I was pulling your leg."

"Well, it wasn't funny." Samantha sighed.

"Well, waking me up wasn't funny," Jessica reminded Samantha. "So I guess that we are even now, aren't we?"

"I guess so." Samantha giggled. "So, how do you know when a tent is waterproof?"

"That's easy. When you buy one, make sure the package says "waterproof." They all should be waterproof, and you should be able to use them straight away without getting wet. I would advise you to take it back if water got in." Jessica smiled.

"How easy is it to put a tent up?" Samantha asked. "I know if I tried to put one up, we would be here all day, so you would have to set off early in the morning just to have it up for that night, and even then it would be very late."

"It's not really that hard to put up a tent, once you get used to it. I was quite sad when I found out that these tents were already up. I was looking forward to putting them up." Jessica sighed.

"Well, I was quite glad when I found that they were up. I think most of us were glad because, like me, they don't know how to put them up." Samantha giggled.

"Well, I was really looking forward to the challenge." Jessica then realised she didn't even know the time. "What time is it, anyway?"

"You were the only one, I think," replied Samantha. "Oh, and before I tell you the time, promise you won't be mad."

"That must mean you don't think I'll be happy." Jessica was worried now; surely Samantha wasn't going to say that it was before six.

"I am not going to tell you the time until you promise," Samantha said, and she meant it. She was very scared that Jessica was going to shout at her when she found out what time it was.

"Okay, I promise. Will you please tell me the time?"

"It's 7:00 a.m.," Samantha said nervously. She wasn't sure what Jessica was going to say. Samantha hoped that she hadn't minded being woken up so early.

"Why did you wake me up so early?" Jessica asked.

"I told you I was bored, and I couldn't be bothered to go and find a book to read." Samantha sighed. "I don't remember packing a book. I wish I had, though."

"Well, I have." Jessica smiled at her friend. "It's over there. If you want to borrow it, you can if you promise to look after it. It's one of my favourite books."

"Thanks, I might borrow it one night to read," Samantha said as she looked around the tent. "There are two things I hate about tents."

"What are they?" Jessica asked, a bit confused.

"One, the space in the tents. There's hardly room to swing a cat." Samantha laughed. "And two, there is no Laura here."

"I agree about the latter one." Jessica missed Laura just as much as Samantha did. They had known one another for ages and wouldn't see one another again for ages. Jessica would see her in the summer holidays. She had wanted to move to Lakeview so she could spend the holidays playing with Samantha, but her mother had said that they couldn't move. The only reason Jessica was okay with it was that it meant she could give Laura all their news.

"Laura wouldn't have been able to come anyway. Wasn't last year her last one?" asked Samantha.

"No, she has one year left," Jessica replied.

"I remember the day we met." Samantha smiled as she thought about it.

"So do I. I thought she was our age, I was shocked when I found out she was two years older."

"So was I. She looked our age that first term, but then the next term, she looked a lot older. I remember her saying our names, and we were like 'Who are you?'" Samantha giggled.

"Oh, I remember that, and she said, 'Don't tease me.'" Jessica continued, "Oh, they were the good old times. I am just glad that the school is still going."

"I think we should go and get washed," Samantha suggested as she looked at her watch again. They had been talking for ten minutes.

Jessica smiled as she unfastened the tent door. "Come on, then, I'm ready."

They made their way down to the lake, where they were told to wash. They washed their hands and faces, then sat around the lake taking in the view for a few minutes before heading back to their tent to get dressed, Samantha in jeans and a pink T-shirt and Jessica in a red skirt and T-shirt, which would be good as she was sure that the sun was going to come out later in the day.

"What should we do now?" Samantha asked as she finished brushing her hair and left the tent.

"I don't know." Jessica sighed. "Are you sure that no one else is up?"

"I can't see anyone." Samantha giggled as she looked around the campsite. "If anyone is awake, then they aren't in camp."

"I didn't see anyone down by the lake," Jessica smiled, "so that would suggest we are the only ones awake."

"Have you decided what we are going to do?"

"Why don't we go for a walk in the woods?" Jessica suggested. "And what time is it?"

"I like that idea," Samantha agreed, then looked at her watch and smiled. "It's 7:25 a.m., so if we go now and be back by 8:00 a.m., I'm sure more people will be up."

"Okay, let's do that then," replied Jessica.

They set off down through the campsite and into the woods. The scenery was great, and they enjoyed listening to the birds singing, and seeing the sunrise in the countryside was great. They had been walking for about half an hour when Samantha suggested that they head back to camp.

"Okay, maybe it would be—" Jessica started to say when she suddenly stepped in a hoop that raised her up into the air.

Samantha, who was walking in front, turned when her friend just stopped talking, and was amazed to find that her friend had disappeared completely. She was annoyed when she couldn't find her, and the only explanation she had was that her friend was playing hide and seek. "Jessica, if you're playing hide and seek, then I give up."

44

Jessica, who was very scared and irritated, shouted, "I'm up here!"

Samantha looked up and saw Jessica. She cheekily asked, "What are you doing up there?"

"I didn't come up here on purpose!" Jessica shouted. "Someone set a trap, and now I'm dangling up here, and I don't like it. Can you please get me down?"

Samantha went to where the rope was wrapped around the tree and quickly tried to untie the knot. "I can't untie the knot."

"Don't tease me, Samantha," shouted Jessica.

"I'm not. I'm being serious. I can't untie the knot," Samantha called up to Jessica.

"So what am I supposed to do then, stay up here all day?" Jessica cried.

"Well, it looks like it."

Jessica was getting scared. She didn't want to have to stay up there much longer, and she was worried that Miss Moore would tell them off for going for a walk on their own. Suddenly Tom and Ben came up to Samantha.

"Seems like we caught someone," laughed Tom.

"You mean, this was your idea?" Samantha said.

"Yes, we thought it would be fun," Ben replied as he untied the knot around the tree.

Jessica fell to the ground, then got up and brushed the leaves and dirt off her skirt and shirt. She never wanted to go through that experience again. "Don't do that again," she snapped as she looked at Ben and Tom.

"Why not?" demanded Tom.

Jessica looked at them and sighed. She liked Tom but didn't like Ben that much. "Because I found it scary."

"Well, we'll think about it," Ben teased.

"I think we should get back to camp," Tom said as he decided that it would be best to change the subject.

"I agree with Tom," Samantha smiled.

"Okay, let's go," Jessica sighed.

Chapter 7

The Mystery Girl

Samantha and Jessica walked back to camp with Tom and Ben. They were hoping they could just sneak in without anyone realising they had gone for a walk. When they got to the edge of the woods, they smiled. It looked like no one was up, but as they got closer, they saw Miss Moore looking for something. They went up to her with smiles on their faces.

"Can we help you?" Samantha asked.

"No, you can't," Miss Moore sighed, "because we are looking for you."

"Why are you looking for us?" Jessica asked.

"Well, we couldn't find you when we got up, and we were worried. Where have you been?"

"We woke up early," Samantha replied, "and I thought that you wouldn't mind us going for a walk so we didn't wake you."

"Well, you could have left a note," snapped Mr. Biggs as he came running up to them.

"We, we didn't—" stammered Jessica as she felt the tears coming, though she tried to be strong and stop the tears.

"Leave this to me," Miss Moore said as she looked at Mr. Biggs.

"Okay, Miss Moore," Mr. Biggs replied as he went off to look after the others.

"You could have left us a note," Miss Moore smiled, "and that way we would have known where you were."

"We didn't think." Samantha answered for the whole group.

"Well, I can see that." Miss Moore sighed.

Tom looked at Miss Moore before saying, "We're sorry."

"I know." Miss Moore smiled. "Why don't we leave it there and get some breakfast? I'm sure that you all must be hungry."

"We are." Ben smiled. "Well, I'm starved."

"Well, you can do the dishes afterwards." Miss Moore laughed. "Can't you?"

"Yes, Miss Moore," they all replied. They didn't really want to wash the dishes, but they knew they had gotten off lightly when they hadn't been punished. They had been scared that Miss Moore would tell their parents what they had done. Samantha knew that she would have been in big trouble and was sure that they would have yelled at her and told her that she had let them down.

"Well, if that is sorted, let's go and get breakfast." Miss Moore smiled as she looked at Samantha. She sensed that Samantha was worried and guessed that the girl was concerned about her telling their parents. "If you wash up, we'll say that's your punishment and nothing more will be said about what you did this morning."

Samantha smiled as she said, "Thank you, Miss Moore."

Miss Moore looked around and saw that everyone else was eating except for them. "Well, don't you think we should get something to eat before they eat it all?"

"Okay," said Jessica.

They all made their way to where Mr. Biggs had started a campfire, then they sat on a log and took the plates that he offered them.

"Thank you, Mr. Biggs," Jessica said.

"Yeah, thank you, Mr. Biggs." Samantha smiled.

They ate the food and then did what they were told; they washed up all the plates and cleaned all the spoons before heading back to the campsite.

Once they got back, Miss Moore looked at them. "Have you finished?"

"Yes, Miss Moore," Jessica replied.

"That is good." Miss Moore smiled at them. "You are just in time for the first activity of the week."

"What we doing?" Ben asked as he looked around the campsite to see if anything might give him an idea of what they were doing.

"We are going on a nature hike to see what we can see, and the one who finds all these animals and plants the quickest will win. And of course they have to bring the sheets back here for me to see. A teacher will be going with each of the four groups to verify what you have seen. The teachers won't help you, but they will be watching you."

"Okay," Jessica said. "Whose team am I on?"

"Well, I thought that you, Ben, Tom, and Samantha would want to be in a team together." Miss Moore smiled. "I am right, am I not?"

"You are, Miss Moore." Samantha giggled. "I always like being partnered with Jessica, and Tom and Ben seem to be nice guys."

"We will have you four together then," Miss Moore said.

"I am glad," Jessica replied, "though may I ask who is going to be our teacher?"

"You will have Mrs. Knight as your guide." Miss Moore looked at them. "If she thinks you need some help and are stuck, then she might help you, though normally she will leave it all up to you four to decide which way to go."

"Okay, Miss Moore." Tom smiled.

"I think you should go. All the other teams have started," Miss Moore said.

They set off on their way to search for Mrs. Knight because they couldn't start without her to prove that they had found everything. They found her sitting at the campfire.

She looked at them as they sat down next to her. "I take it I have to follow you lot around," she said.

"Yes, Mrs. Knight." Jessica smiled back.

"Well, I think we had best be off," Mrs. Knight said as she got up from her seat. "The other groups started out about ten minutes ago."

"I agree," said Samantha. "We will have to work hard to catch up."

They all got up and headed toward the beautiful woods. Jessica and Ben wanted to stay there and find what they could, but Samantha suggested they continue because she couldn't see how they would find the things on the list otherwise. Samantha and Jessica were walking together and took a wrong turn; they walked for five minutes before realising anything was wrong.

"What time is it?" Jessica suddenly asked Samantha.

"It's—" started Samantha as she looked at her watch, "I don't know what time it is, because it seems that my watch has stopped."

"Well, maybe Tom or Ben knows the time." Jessica smiled as she turned around to ask them. She was startled, as there was no sign of Tom, Ben, or Mrs. Knight.

"Samantha, I don't want to scare you, but there's no sign of the others," Jessica said calmly. She knew that Samantha would freak out.

"What!" shouted Samantha. "You're joking, right?"

"No, I am not joking. They're nowhere in sight," replied Jessica.

"Well, they can't be far, can they?" Samantha asked as she turned around to make sure that the boys weren't there. She was sure that Jessica must be playing a trick on her.

"Do you believe me now?" Jessica asked as she saw Samantha looking around. "Or do you want to look again just to make sure?"

"Yes, I believe you." Samantha sighed. She knew that they had somehow lost the others and wondered if they had realised that the girls were missing. Surely they should have.

***

Meanwhile, the boys and Mrs. Knight were trying to figure out what on the list to look for first; they couldn't decide what would be the best thing to find.

"Girls, what do you think we should do?" Tom thought that the girls were being very quiet, so he decided to ask them for suggestions.

"Yeah, girls, you must have some ideas on how we can sort this out." Ben laughed. "You're not telling me you're shy?"

When there was no answer, they turned around and realised that the girls had somehow disappeared.

"They could be anywhere in the wood." Tom sighed.

"What are we going to do? We can't go back to Miss Moore and tell her that we have lost Jessica and Samantha.

She would tell us off for not keeping an eye on them, and she would surely tell Mrs. Knight off for not looking after us more. See, she is over there asleep. I haven't seen anyone sleep so much in my entire life." Ben laughed as he looked around at Mrs. Knight.

"I seriously think we should wake her up," Tom suggested. "She should know because if we don't find them, she will be the one in the most trouble. She is the teacher and should have been watching us."

"Okay, I think you're right." Ben smiled.

They went up to Mrs. Knight and gentle tried to wake her up but couldn't. They tried everything from poking her to singing to well, just about everything they could think of. The only thing they didn't do—and that was because they would have been in a lot of trouble—was the idea of chucking a bucket of water on Mrs. Knight, and that was only because Tom wouldn't let Ben do it.

"Wake up, sleepy head!" Tom screamed as loudly as he could.

"Wake up, Mrs. Knight!" Ben also screamed.

The screaming together had the effect they wanted. Mrs. Knight woke up, but it took her a few moments to remember where she was.

"Where are the girls?" she asked as she remembered that when they had started out there had been five of them. "And how are you doing on the nature walk?"

"We aren't doing very well. We are rubbish at finding animal and plants, and we wouldn't be able to find them even if we looked until midnight." Ben was deliberately trying to ignore the first question; he couldn't decide what he would tell Mrs. Knight about the girls being missing.

"Where are the girls?" Mrs. Knight asked again.

Tom decided that the best thing to do was to tell her, then quickly change the subject. "We don't know," he said really fast, then added, "Lovely weather we are having."

"What was that?" Mrs, Knight said as she caught onto what Tom was trying to do.

"I said it's lovely weather that we are having today." Tom smiled.

"No, before that. You said something about the girls." Mrs. Knight was getting annoyed. "I want an honest answer, and I want it now."

"He said they were missing," Ben said as he realised that Tom wasn't going to tell her what he had said.

"I thought he did." Mrs. Knight sighed. "I have no idea what we are going to do."

"I think we should go and look for them," suggested Tom.

"You are right." Mrs Knight smiled. "Unfortunately, it will probably mean that we will have no chance of finding everything on the list, unless I say you have, even though you haven't, in turn for you not telling Miss Moore that I fell asleep instead of making sure that you and the girls were safe and together."

"No, I think that we will just tell the truth," Tom said. "That's the best way."

"But I could lose my job," Mrs Knight cried.

"Well, we could just say they took a wrong turn and we didn't realise," Ben suggested. "I think that will be the best way."

"I like that idea." The others smiled.

***

"We're totally lost," cried Samantha. "Whatever will we do?"

"We have to keep calm." Jessica smiled.

"Keep calm! We're in the middle of nowhere! And all you say is 'keep calm'!" Samantha shouted at the top of her voice. "We could be trapped here for ages."

"We won't be. The first thing people tell you is that when you are lost, you have to keep—" Jessica started, then stopped. She was sure she was seeing things...well, if she wasn't, they were in big trouble, as a woman in a long, red coat was pointing at them as if to say, "Follow me." "Do you see what I see?"

"I do." Samantha smiled. "I think we should follow her; she seems to know her way around."

"You know what Miss Moore says about following strangers," Jessica reminded Samantha. "She says that if you don't know them, the best thing to do is just leave."

"Well, you can leave, but I'm following her." Samantha smiled.

"You're crazy then." Jessica sighed.

"I just have this feeling that everything will be safe with her," Samantha replied. "Please trust me on this. I am sure that she will lead us back to camp."

"Okay, I'll trust you," Jessica replied. "But don't say I didn't warn you if anything goes wrong."

"Okay, that's a deal." Samantha smiled.

Chapter 8

The House Across from Camp

The woman smiled as she realised that the girls were going to follow her. She had no intention of harming them; she just wanted to see them safely back to their campsite, as there were a lot of wild animals in the woods. The two of them on their own in the woods could have been dangerous, and she didn't want anything to happen to these two lovely girls. She smiled as they got nearer, but before they could see her face or say thank you, she quickly turned around and started to walk toward their campsite.

"I have a bad feeling," Jessica said again. "I just know that something is going to happen."

"I told you, I am sure that nothing will happen to us; in fact, I have a feeling that I know this woman from somewhere, but I just can't place my finger on where it is." Samantha smiled as she linked arms with her friend. "I tell you there is nothing to worry about."

"If there's nothing to worry about, why won't she speak to us instead of walking in silence?" Jessica asked.

"Maybe she has lost her voice," Samantha blurted out.

"I doubt it." Jessica giggled.

"Well, you never know." Samantha laughed.

They decided to stop talking then because the lady turned around as if to try to tell them to keep up. They walked for half an hour before they finally exited the woods. Samantha and Jessica hoped that it wouldn't be too far away from their camp, so they were surprised when they were actually at the site. They looked around but couldn't see anyone.

"I told you we would get back to the campsite safely." Samantha smiled. "I told you we had nothing to worry about."

"Okay, so you were right. We didn't have anything to worry about." Jessica added, "But you do realise that we could have been in serious trouble if that woman had taken us anywhere else. We wouldn't have been able to find our way back here, or worse—we wouldn't have been able to defend ourselves. If my parents find out, I will be in so much trouble."

"Well, we just won't tell them then," Samantha said quickly and thoughtfully. "I am just curious to know who that woman was. I'm sure I know her."

Samantha and Jessica turned to the woman to thank her, but all they could see was the entrance to the woods. The woman had just disappeared into thin air, and they hoped she was okay.

Samantha turned to Jessica before saying, "Now, that's strange."

"I know," Jessica replied. "She didn't even wait for us to thank her."

Samantha was just about to reply when Miss Moore came up to them with a smile on her face, but that soon disappeared when she realised that Tom and Ben weren't with them.

"Hello, Miss Moore," Jessica said as she nudged Samantha, who was looking down at her shoe.

Samantha quickly looked up when she felt the nudge, and she was scared when she saw Miss Moore. Was she about to be told off for leaving her group? "Hello, Miss Moore."

"Where are Mrs. Knight and the boys in your group?" Miss Moore asked. She wasn't in the mood for any cheek. She needed to make sure everything was okay.

"We don't know," Samantha cried.

"Jessica, you had better tell me what is going on and why Samantha is upset," Miss Moore said sweetly.

"Well, you see, Miss, it's quite simple. We have no idea where the boys or Mrs. Knight are, because we lost them. It seems that we took a wrong turn," Jessica replied.

"Well, at least you had sense to come back here when you got lost." Miss Moore smiled. "I am proud of you both."

Samantha and Jessica looked at each other. They were both wondering if they should tell Miss Moore what had happened but decided against it.

"I think you should come and join me by the lake." Miss Moore smiled as she looked at them. She really was proud of them; the person she was upset with was Mrs. Knight. Why hadn't she come back and told her that Samantha and Jessica were missing?

"We would love to." Samantha smiled.

They set off down to the lake, sat on the edge of it, and took their shoes and socks off to soak their feet. The ice-cold water was refreshing.

Samantha looked across the lake and saw a house. "Who owns that house?" she asked Miss Moore.

"No one. I have a story about that house I want to tell, but I want to tell everyone, so I'll tell you all tonight." Miss Moore smiled.

"Oh, can't you tell us now?" Jessica begged.

"I'm sorry, Jessica, you will have to wait until tonight."

"Okay, I'll wait." Jessica sighed.

"Well, that's good. The best things always happen to those who wait." Miss Moore laughed. "I got taught that when I was at school quite awhile back now."

"We'll wait," Samantha said quietly.

***

In the junior camp they were having fun. Most of the children were in their bathing suits so that they could have a swim. Becky, who had been swimming, looked up and saw Mr. Baker. She swam over to ask him a question.

"Who does that house over there belong to?"

"It belongs to me, my wife, and Samantha," Mr. Baker replied.

"What do you mean, Mr. Baker?" Becky asked.

"I mean that I bought the house so that my wife, my lovely daughter, and I could live in it; it's not that far away from the school, only about one hour's drive," Mr. Baker said.

"But it took the bus more than an hour to get here, so how can it take you only one hour to get to the school, when that is farther away from the school than we are?" Becky demanded.

"Well, you see, there is a road that the house attaches to." Mr. Baker smiled at Becky. "And that comes out further down the main road than this does, plus a car can go a lot faster than a bus, because a car isn't as big as a bus." He looked at Becky before adding, "Do you understand me?"

"Yes, Mr. Baker," Becky replied as she adjusted the top of her red bathing suit.

"I think that you should go and enjoy yourself," Mr. Baker said with a smile, "because we will be doing something else soon."

"Okay, Mr. Baker," Becky said as she turned to go out and swim for a bit more. She also wanted to tell the others what Mr. Baker had said.

"Oh, and one last thing. What I have told you, I don't want anyone else knowing because I don't want Samantha to find out. The more students who know, the more likely it will be that she does." Mr. Baker smiled kindly.

"Okay, Mr. Baker," Becky promised. "I won't tell anyone else."

"There's a good girl." Mr. Baker smiled at her. "Now go on and enjoy yourself with your mates. I can see that they are waiting for you."

Becky smiled as she looked around. "They are great friends, and they always wait for me." She quickly went to where the group was waiting for her.

Mr. Baker smiled. She reminded him of Jessica and Samantha at her age. They also had been waiting for one another. Becky's friends seemed like they would wait as long as was necessary, just like Samantha and Jessica.

***

Mrs. Knight, Tom, and Ben were still in the woods looking for Jessica and Samantha. They had no idea that the girls were now safely back at camp.

"What should we do?" Tom suddenly asked Mrs. Knight.

"I think we had better go and tell Miss Moore that we have lost Samantha and Jessica. I just hope she isn't too cross with us." Mrs. Knight sighed.

"I agree," Ben said. "I think we have searched everywhere we can think of." He looked at the others before adding, "It's time to let Miss Moore look for them."

"Okay, we'll do that then," Mrs Knight said sadly. She was sure that she would be in trouble for losing them. "Come on."

They made their way back, and it seemed like the whole of the camp was there. Everyone had finished the nature walk and was eating dinning, including Samantha and Jessica. Mrs. Knight was shocked when she saw them.

She walked over to them and smiled. "When did you get back?"

"We got back a while ago. We got separated and thought that the best thing would be to come back to camp." Samantha smiled.

"Why didn't you come and tell us Samantha and Jessica had gotten lost?" Miss Moore suddenly asked Mrs. Knight.

"I thought that I could deal with it," Mrs Knight replied.

"Well, next time come and find me and tell me."

"I will do," Mrs. Knight said calmly.

"We'll leave it there then," Miss Moore said.

They all sat down to eat their dinner. The rest of the day was spent having fun. The juniors had a go at pottery making and the seniors went for a swim in the lake. It was 5:00 p.m. when they left the pond to get cleaned off; no one could be bothered to get changed for tea, so they sat around on the grass in their swimming costumes whilst they ate.

Once they were finished, Jessica looked at Miss Moore and smiled. "Can we have that story now, please?"

"Don't you want to get changed first?" Miss Moore suggested. "It's going to be cold tonight, and I'm sure that those swimming costumes must be wet through."

They did what Miss Moore suggested. By the time they were ready for Miss Moore to tell them the story, it was already seven o'clock.

"Okay, this is a story about that house over there." Miss Moore pointed at it. "You see, this camp and that house were part of the same property. The owner of the house had seen how bored his daughters were during the summer, even though they had a lake to go down and swim in every day. Even that gets boring after awhile, so his butler came up with an idea to keep the girls happy."

"What was the idea?" Samantha interrupted, as she was eager to find out.

"Well, it's quite simple. The idea was to build a camp for the girls to invite their friends over to." Miss Moore looked around before continuing. "The camp was so popular with the girls' friends that he decided the best thing to do would be to have two camps, one for the girls and their friends, which is the campsite that we are at now, and one for the public."

"What happened to the campsite?" Samantha interrupted.

"When the girls grew up, their father couldn't bring himself to come here. He kept the public camp going strong until he died. It is said that his ghost haunts the house, and that is why no one lives there," Miss Moore said.

"Well, I wouldn't mind living there," Jessica said. "I'm not scared of any ghost."

"Well now I think we should do something else before we go to bed," Clare suggested. She really didn't like ghosts.

"Okay, Clare, we will do something else." Miss Moore smiled.

They played some games and roasted some marshmallows, which tasted delicious, then went to bed for what they thought would be a good night's sleep. They were all soon fast asleep and dreaming of different things. They had no idea that the peaceful night was about to be shattered.

Chapter 9

What Is Going On?

Samantha, who had been sleeping peacefully, was woken up when a light shined on her tent. It took her awhile to remember where she was, and when she did remember, she wondered where the light was coming from. She took out her watch that Miss Moore had mended for her earlier and looked at the time; it was only one o'clock in the morning. Samantha decided not to wake up Jessica and instead opened the tent and looked around to see if she could see the light source. She looked at the house and was amazed that a light was on. She screamed as loudly as she could; surely, the ghost story wasn't true.

The whole camp woke up when Samantha screamed, they all quickly got out of their tents to see what the matter was with Samantha.

"What's the matter?" Clare asked. "And where is that light coming from?"

"Look over there." Samantha pointed toward the house.

They all looked across the lake and screamed, Clare the loudest.

"It's the ghost," Clare shouted.

"Don't be silly," Miss Moore said, though she was just as worried as the children were. "I think the best thing to do is to go back to bed."

They all agreed, and as the light soon turned off, there was no trouble in them getting back to sleep, although Clare, who hated ghosts, couldn't get back to sleep until four o'clock.

They all woke up late on Monday morning, and even Samantha, who usually was up and ready around six o'clock, wasn't awake until nine o'clock.

Samantha awoke suddenly and looked at her watch. She quickly got dressed and looked around at Jessica. "Wake up, sleepy head."

Jessica woke when Samantha spoke to her. "What time is it?"

"It's 9:20," Samantha replied. "We are lazy today. I am sure that all the others will have had breakfast already. I just hope they have saved us some."

"We are up late." Jessica got out of her bed and sighed. Surely the others would have saved them some breakfast.

Once they were ready, they got out of their tent and were surprised to see that there was nobody else around except for Miss Moore, who sat on her own near the campfire. They sat down next to her.

"Good morning, girls," Miss Moore said without looking at them.

"Good morning, Miss Moore." Samantha smiled. "Where is everyone else?"

"They are still in bed," she replied. "I thought it would be best to allow everyone to sleep in after what happened last night."

Samantha blushed. She regretted screaming the way she did. "I'm sorry I screamed, Miss Moore. I just was so scared."

"It's okay, Samantha. I would have done the same thing." Jessica giggled.

"Yeah, Samantha, there's nothing to worry about." Miss Moore smiled. "Why don't we have breakfast?"

"I would love some. I'm so hungry," Samantha said quietly.

So they ate their breakfast, and soon the whole camp was up, including Clare. They soon dressed and were ready for the activity that Miss Moore had planned.

"Today you will be in the same groups as yesterday for a treasure hunt." Miss Moore smiled. "We have hidden thing around the woods, and here is the list of everything you have to find."

She handed everyone a list, and they were soon busy heading toward the woods. Samantha and Jessica had no intention of doing the hunt; they wanted to investigate the house across the lake.

"Come on, Jessica." Samantha smiled as they thought the boys had gone ahead.

They were just about to go when Tom said, "Where do you think you two are going?"

"We are going to investigate the house. You see, when we were lost, this woman helped us, and Samantha is sure that she and the house are connected," replied Jessica.

"Well, we are coming with you this time," Ben said.

"What about Mrs. Knight?" Samantha asked.

"She's asleep and won't wake up for awhile yet." Tom smiled. "She always has to take a rest after walking a little bit."

"Wow, that's so odd. I hope she's okay." Jessica replied.

"I think we should get going." Samantha said.

"Okay, we're right behind you two," Tom said as he watched Samantha turn to leave. "You do know your way, I assume."

"Well, we were thinking of sneaking back to camp and changing into our swimming costumes so we could swim across the lake. It really doesn't seem so far," Jessica whispered. She was sure that the boys wouldn't like the idea.

"What? Are you out—?" started Tom, but Ben cut across him.

"We'll come with you." He had been bored for the past few days and thought that the idea of going to the house that was supposed to be haunted was a dream come true.

"Okay, then, we had better go," Samantha said quietly.

They quickly left the woods and were soon back at the camp. They were glad when they didn't see Miss Moore anywhere.

"Meet back here in ten minutes," Samantha suggested.

They all agreed that would be a good idea and were soon getting their swimming costumes on. Ten minutes later they were back at the meeting point.

"I'm ready." Samantha smiled.

"Are you sure this is safe?" Tom asked.

"Of course we are. Do you think we would be doing something that isn't safe?" Samantha laughed as she went to the edge of the lake and dived in. The icy water touched her skin and she felt cold but knew that, once she started to swim, she would warm up.

Ben and Jessica followed her in, and had already set off when Tom decided that he would give it a try. He hated swimming, but he didn't want to miss out on the fun.

"Wait for me," he said as he finally dived into the water.

The other three stopped and waited for him to catch up.

"I was sure that you weren't going to come," Samantha said wickedly.

"Well, I wasn't, but then I thought that if I let you three go, you could get into trouble," Tom replied. "I wouldn't have been able to look at Miss Moore again if anything happened to you."

"Well, I am glad you have decided to come," Jessica said as she hugged him. "Now let's set off before anyone sees us."

They looked around and realised that they were right in the line of sight for the camp, and if anyone had been looking, they surely would have seen the children in the lake. They set off as fast as they could. The water was cold, and it was hard to reach the other side, but they made it after about forty minutes.

"What a lovely place." Jessica smiled as she got out of the lake. "I wouldn't mind living here."

"Neither would I," Samantha replied as she looked around the grounds. There were loads of lovely flowers all over the place and also quite a few unique-looking trees. Samantha was sure that she would have loved living in a place like that, plus the house had what looked like four floors.

"This is one big house." Tom sighed. "Even I have to admit that the swim was worth it just to see a house so beautiful."

"Shall we go in?" Ben suggested.

"Do you think that is wise?" Samantha asked worriedly. She hadn't wanted to go into the house, just see whether the woman lived there.

"I think it's a good idea." Jessica said.

"Well, if you're sure." Samantha sighed.

Ben led them up the pathway to the house, and when they got there, he opened the door quietly in case anyone was at home. He was a bit nervous; he had a funny feeling that something wasn't quite right.

Jessica, who had been standing behind Samantha, suddenly tapped her shoulders.

"What's the matter, Jessica?" Samantha asked as she turned around to look at her friend.

"I really think that you should see this." Jessica was as white as a ghost.

"See what?" Samantha replied as she realised that her friend was scared.

"I really think you should see this," Jessica said as she pointed to a picture on the wall.

The others turned around and looked. At first they couldn't see what was worrying her so much since it was just a picture of a girl about their age. It was Tom who realised what was bothering Jessica.

"Doesn't she remind you of someone, Samantha?" he asked as he turned to look at her. She seemed to be struggling to recognise who it was.

Suddenly a light when off in her head as she realised who it was. "I know her. She's a great friend of mine." She decided that she would tease the others.

"I think you know her better than that," Ben replied.

"I know." Samantha giggled. "She looks exactly like me."

They all wondered who this mystery girl was who looked so much like Samantha.

"I think we should move," Jessica suggested. "Seeing Samantha on the wall is making me nervous."

"It's making me worried," Samantha and Tom both said at the same time, Samantha lying of course.

They all made their way into the living room and Samantha stopped dead. There were pictures of her mother and father on the wall and also the piano that was going to their new house.

"Samantha, what is going on?" Tom blurted out.

"I have no idea," Samantha replied seriously, she knew full well what was going on but wanted to tease her friends. "This is beginning to freak me out."

"It's beginning to freak us all out," Tom replied.

Suddenly the lights went on and there was a figure at the door.

***

Mrs. Knight was beginning to awake from her sleep.

"I wonder where the children are." She sighed as she remembered that she should have been looking after them whilst they were on their treasure hunt.

Mrs. Knight looked around the entire forest before realising that they weren't anywhere to be seen. She knew she must tell Miss Moore, but she was scared of telling her that she had fallen asleep when the children had gone missing.

***

At the camp, all the other teams had come back and were enjoying their dinner, though Miss Moore was really worried about Samantha, Jessica, et al., because the others had been back for a while.

"I wonder where Mrs. Knight's group is," she said to the other staff.

"I'm sure that they are okay." Mr Biggs smiled back at her.

"Well, I hope you're right," Miss Moore said.

Mrs. Knight, who had been running all the way back to camp, suddenly came into view and startled Miss Moore.

Miss Moore was just about to ask the children if they had collected everything on the list when she realised that they weren't with Mrs. Knight. "Where are the children?"

"I was hoping they would be back here," Mrs Knight replied truthfully.

"Well, they aren't." Miss Moore sighed. "Are you telling me that you have lost them?"

"Well, yes, you see we were walking together, and the next thing I remember was asking them a question, and they weren't there," lied Mrs. Knight. She wasn't going to tell Miss Moore that she had fallen asleep whilst she was on duty."

"We had better find them," Mr Biggs suddenly suggested.

"I think that would be the best plan." Mrs. Knight sighed.

"Is there anywhere they might have gone?" Miss Show asked. She had been seated quietly and normally spoke only when anyone spoke to her.

"Well, there's her father." Miss Moore smiled. "Do you think they could have gone to see him?" She wasn't sure if Samantha would have.

"It's worth a try." Mr Biggs sighed, he really hated all the worry that Samantha had been causing since they had come on the camping trip.

"You can go and see Mr. Baker whilst we all go and search the woods," Miss Moore said.

"You don't think they would have gone over to the house after what happened last night?" Miss Show suddenly suggested.

"No, I don't think they would have." Miss Moore thought that would have been least likely, so she continued with the plan for Mr. Biggs going to see Mr. Baker and the others searching the woods.

Chapter 10

A Puzzling Thought

Samantha and Jessica were scared when the woman turned on the lights.

"What are you doing in this house?" the woman asked.

"We're lost and were wondering if the owner would help us." Samantha sighed. "We didn't mean to cause any trouble, and we really are sorry for bursting in. We should have knocked, I know."

The woman froze when she heard Samantha's voice. It was the last thing she had expected to hear. "Samantha, is that you?"

"Yes, it is." Samantha looked at the woman who was in the room. "Cook! What on earth are you doing here?"

"I'll get your mum so she can explain," Cook replied.

Cook went off upstairs, and Ben wanted to run for it, but Samantha and Jessica stopped him. They were curious as to why Samantha's mother was in a house so huge. Mrs. Baker came downstairs with a smile on her face.

"Samantha, Jessica, it's so nice to see you."

"Hi, Mrs. Baker." Jessica smiled as she looked at Mrs. Baker.

"Mother, it was you who helped me and Jessica yesterday, wasn't it? Come on, please tell us, because I had a feeling I recognised her," Samantha blurted out, hoping her mother wouldn't be cross with her. Then, remembering her manners, she smiled as she said, "Oh, and hello."

"Yes, I was the one to help you out." Mrs Baker smiled.

"I am glad that it was you, but like I told Jessica, I was sure that we could trust the person, but she was saying we shouldn't follow you, and I was like, it's the only way we are going to get back because we have no idea where the campsite is, even though Miss Moore told us to study where about on the map we were." Samantha said happily, "I told you, Jessica, nothing bad would happen."

"Well, I didn't know it was your mother." Jessica giggled. "But I am glad that we followed you, Mrs. Baker, because otherwise I think we would have been looking for the campsite now. As Samantha just said, we had no idea where the campsite is."

Mrs. Baker sighed as she listened to Samantha and Jessica and looked at the girls. "Well, how are you getting back now?" Mrs. Baker knew the way for them to get back, but she wanted them to know what they did was wrong.

Jessica smiled, "We could swim back."

"You could, I admit, but I won't let you, anything could happen," said Mrs. Baker. She then suddenly remembered something. "Well, Samantha, you have spoilt the surprise that we were going to give you."

"Oh, I'm sorry, but we were told a story about this house being haunted, and then when we saw a light on last night, we thought it would be fun to investigate what was going on," Samantha said. "I tell you one thing; I really wasn't expecting to see you."

"Well, you have seen me." Mrs. Baker laughed as she hugged her daughter and then realised that she was just in her swimming costume. "I think, Samantha, you should change, and you too, Jessica, but I'm afraid I don't have any clothes for the boys."

They went upstairs, Samantha let Jessica borrow a skirt and a T-shirt, and then they went downstairs to where Mrs. Baker was lighting a fire for them.

"I assume that you all must be cold." Mrs. Baker smiled warmly.

"Yes, I think I can speak for us all when I say that we are," Ben replied as he sat down in front of the fire to try to get himself warmer.

"I also assume that Miss Moore doesn't know that you are here," Mrs. Baker said as she watched the children sit down in front of the fire.

Samantha looked at her mother. "We didn't have time."

"She means *no*, Miss," Tom replied.

"Well, I am ashamed of you all. Anything could have happened to you."

"We're sorry," Jessica cried.

"I'll go and see the maid and tell her to look after you whilst I go and tell Miss Moore where you are," Mrs. Baker said. "Whilst I am gone, Cook will make you all a nice cup of hot chocolate."

"Thanks, Mother." Samantha smiled as she gave her mother a hug.

Mrs. Baker looked at her daughter as she hugged her. She was about to leave the room when she suddenly stopped and turned around, "How on Earth did you get here?"

"We swam across the lake," Jessica said.

"That must have taken you ages." Mrs. Baker was in total shock. She had no idea how far it was from one end of the lake to the other, but it looked pretty far, and she was sure it must have taken them awhile to swim it.

"It didn't take us that long." Samantha protested, even though she knew this was a lie. "It took around twenty minutes."

"Well, you must be tired," Mrs. Baker said, ignoring the fact that Samantha had said it hadn't taken them long. She knew what her daughter was like.

"We are a bit," Tom said.

"I'll be back as soon as I can." Mrs. Baker smiled as she finally left the room.

Cook came in and brought them all a drink of hot chocolate; they were soon settled in front of the fire drinking their hot chocolate.

***

Mr. Biggs had finally made it to where the juniors were staying. Mr. Baker ran up when he saw him.

"Hello, Mr. Biggs. What a surprise." Mr Baker smiled as he held out his hand.

"Hello, Mr. Baker. I need to ask you a question," Mr. Biggs replied as they shook hands.

"What can I do for you?" Mr. Baker was quite curious as to what was happening in the senior camp.

"Have you seen your daughter today?" Mr. Biggs blurted out.

"No. Should I have?" Mr. Baker was surprised.

"Well, we haven't seen her since we started the treasure hunt. She and a few friends have gone missing," Mr. Biggs said.

"Who are the others?" Mr. Baker was scared now.

"The others are Tom, Ben, and Jessica," Mr. Biggs said calmly.

"I think the best thing to do would be to look around the woods," Mr. Baker suggested.

"Well, if you think it would help." Mr. Biggs sighed.

Mr. Baker went up to the other junior teachers and smiled. "Mr. Brown, I am going to leave you in charge whilst I go and help search for a senior."

"Okay, Mr. Baker." Mr. Brown smiled; he was glad that he was being left in charge.

Miss Lionheart was more concerned with the missing students. "Do you want me to help you search for them?"

"No, we need you to stay behind and look after the juniors. We don't want them thinking that something is up; it would spoil their trip," Mr. Baker said. "But thanks for the offer."

Mr. Baker and Mr. Biggs went off into the woods and searched high and low. They looked up the trees and even went into an abandoned tree house, but there wasn't any sight of the missing children.

"I think we should go back to the senior camp," Mr. Biggs suggested.

"That's the best idea. Maybe the others have had more luck," Mr. Baker said sadly.

They made their way back to the camp past trees and fallen logs that were blocking their paths. It was really hard finding their way to the senior camp, but they managed, and as soon as they got there, they realised that none of the others had had any luck.

"Any luck?" Miss Moore asked in desperation.

"No, there was no sign that they had been in the woods," Mr. Baker said, knowing that Miss Moore must have been going through a lot.

Miss Show came running up to them. "I had a look in their tents whilst you were away and their swimming costumes are gone."

"Are you serious?" Miss Moore sighed. She had been dreading being told that because it meant anything could have happened.

"I hope they haven't drowned." Mr. Biggs looked shocked.

"I'm very serious," Miss Show said.

"I think we might have to go down to the police station and tell them what has happened. We haven't been here three days and already we have had a disappearance. Surely this isn't going to go down too well with the parents." Miss Moore sighed. "I have half a mind to cancel the school and get a job that is less stressful."

"But then what would you do?" Mr Clarke asked with a twinkle in his eyes.

"I would manage somehow," Miss Moore started but then she changed tones once she saw the look on Mr. Baker's face. "Okay, so I wouldn't manage. I was born to run a school, and I don't think I could go back to being just a head teacher after running a school, especially one like this."

"I thought you would feel that way." Mr. Clarke laughed.

"Should I go down to the police station?" Miss Show asked.

"Yes, I think that would be—" Miss Moore broke off when she saw a car coming down the road to the campsite. It parked right next to the bus, and the driver got out. The woman ran all the way down to the lot of them.

"Mrs. Baker!" Miss Moore exclaimed. "What a surprise."

"Hello, Miss Moore."

"What are you doing here?" Miss Moore asked.

"I came to tell you that the missing students are at my house." Mrs. Baker smiled as she looked at the group, who seemed to be in total shock.

"But you're staying in a hotel room, aren't you?" Miss Moore was surprised to hear that the students had gone all the way to where Mr. and Mrs. Baker were staying.

"Not anymore. I was moving our stuff into the house across the lake when they came walking in. They said someone told them a ghost was living there, and they wanted to see it." Mrs. Baker sighed.

Miss Moore blushed. "That would be me."

"Well, don't tell them that anymore." Mrs. Baker laughed.

"I'll come with you to collect them." Miss Moore smiled.

"So will I," Mr. Baker said to his wife.

They made their way to the Bakers' car and then drove the ten miles that it took them to get to the house. Once they were there, Miss Moore was amazed at how beautiful the house was, and she was hoping that she could visit it a few times. They made their way to the room that the children were in.

"Hi, Miss Moore," the children said as they saw her enter the room.

"Hi, children." She smiled as she looked at them.

"We are sorry we ran off." Jessica sighed.

"That's good." Miss Moore said. "Now, hurry up. Mrs. Baker has kindly agreed to drive us all back to the camp. Ben, Tom, and Jessica, come with me, and Samantha and Mr. Baker will come later."

"Okay." Samantha sighed as she said goodbye to the others. "See you back at camp."

It took them more than two hours to get the whole lot back to camp, and Mrs. Baker decided that she would stay and have some tea with them before she left.

Samantha was the first to talk. "Do you think that we will have any more adventures?"

"After the first few days of this camping trip, I hope that we can now settle down and have a peaceful term," Miss Moore said calmly.

"I doubt it." Mrs. Baker smiled. "And for the record, it's the school building that is supposed to be haunted. Apparently, the building was used by three brothers to steal trophies and money, trophies from a competition called the Quiz Challenge." Mrs. Baker looked at Miss Moore, who had gone white. "The three brothers apparently lost their lives in a fire, but they still guard their ill-gotten gold."

"Well, I hope we don't see them." Samantha giggled. She loved ghost stories, but this one was just stupid, and why Miss Moore had gone white she had no idea. She had forgotten about the article that she, Jessica, and Laura had seen. Jessica hadn't, though, and she made a note to talk to Samantha. She was hoping that Laura was okay; the day after they read the article, they hadn't seen Laura, and the next day they had phoned her to say unfortunately they wouldn't be able to see her until the end of summer, as they had stuff to do before they got to camp and the fact that Laura had told them she was going to visit family so she wouldn't be able to talk to them until September at the earliest.

Chapter 11

News from Jessica

Jessica was glad that the school term had started the day after camp, because her mother had come up the night before with some news. Jessica had stayed in a hotel that night; she was upset about what she had been told and shown.

"Jessica," a voice said from behind. "We're in the same dorm, and there are a few other girls in our dorm," Samantha said as she hugged her best friend. "The boys have their own dorm at the other end of the building." Samantha had heard this from her dad. "We will be having math first thing tomorrow." Then, looking at Jessica's face, she asked, "What's wrong?"

Jessica hadn't realised that her face was showing how upset she was. "I'll tell you later." She smiled. "I don't want everyone to hear."

Samantha was wondering what was wrong with Jessica, but she knew not to push the subject, and if Jessica didn't want everyone to know, then Samantha would just wait until there weren't so many people around who could eavesdrop on the conversation. She had an idea that she should get Jessica thinking about something else.

"Jessica, why don't we go for a walk? We can't do anything until everyone has gotten here, and those coming on the train won't be getting here for at least another hour. It won't be until 4:00 p.m. that we all go to the dining hall and listen to what Miss Moore has to say. The juniors won't be there; they have their own dining hall in their building." Samantha smiled. "The only time we will see them is when everyone has free time on Sundays."

Jessica laughed. "That seems cool. At least the juniors get to come over here on a Sunday. That will be good for the older girls and boys who have younger sisters or brothers in the junior section."

"I think that is why Miss Moore decided to allow the younger children to come over on Sunday. I have to tell you what I have heard." Samantha then whispered into Jessica's ear something that she didn't want anyone else to hear.

"I get where you're coming from." Jessica smiled as she stroked her head. "And don't worry, I promise that I won't tell anyone." She looked at her friend and then remembered something. "I am sure that you said we were going for a walk."

Samantha laughed and nudged her friend. "And so we are. We just got talking, that was all. Or don't you like talking?" Samantha winked.

"Of course I like talking, but I also like walking." Jessica laughed as she realised that Samantha was messing with her. "I've just got here and would like to see what the grounds are like."

"Oh, yeah, you won't have seen them yet." Samantha had almost forgotten. Turning to another girl, she smiled. "If Mrs. Baker comes looking for a Samantha, please tell her that she is outside having a walk."

The other girl smiled. "Okay, I'll do that. I'm Olivia Spence, and I take it you're Samantha." She held out her hand for Samantha to shake.

Samantha shook hands with Olivia and then said, "Nice to meet you, Olivia. I think you're in mine and Jessica's dorm." She pointed at Jessica, who said hi to Olivia. "I'll talk to you later. I want to get this walk going, and I see you're busy."

"Yeah, I'm sorting my things out." Olivia smiled. Her long blonde hair was messy after the ride to the school. "After that, I'm going to tidy my hair." Olivia was tall and thin with shiny blue eyes and wore her hair in a ponytail.

Samantha and Jessica left Olivia in the cloak room and went out the side door, the front door being out of bounds to students, as that was how the parents and other important people came into the school. Miss Moore didn't want them being disturbed by all the students. Once they were outside, Samantha looked at Jessica and wondered if she should now ask what was wrong with her. Instead, she pointed to a patch of the school grounds. "That is where a garden club will be run by a teacher. They will plant flowers and fruit trees and some vegetables."

"That sounds cool." Jessica looked to where Samantha was pointing. "Maybe we could join the club when it gets started. I'm sure your parents would want you to, and I think it would be interesting to see what you have to do." Jessica looked straight at Samantha and decided it was time to tell her what was wrong. "Samantha, I have some news." She fished in her pocket until she came across a newspaper clipping from a few months back. "I think you should read this."

Samantha took the piece of paper that Jessica was holding and then started to read it. Once she took the letter, she knew at once what was wrong. Laura's mother had been in touch.

***

Girl Missing

Laura Thompson, a local schoolgirl, has disappeared. Laura had just changed schools from Moore Field School for Girls to Milton High School.

Laura had been asked by teacher Jonathan Walker to speak to him about some work she had handed in, said goodbye to her mates, and went with the teacher toward the school building. Neither she nor Walker has been seen since. There is reason to believe that something could have happened to them both.

The headmaster of the school had this to say: "This is a very unique situation that hasn't happened before, and I want to promise the parents that a full investigation will be happening and we will be cooperating with the police."

The police sergeant in charge of finding Laura added, "We will do all in our powers to find Laura and make sure that she is brought back to her family. We will be looking into the history of this teacher to find out if he is involved in this situation, or if he, like Laura, was just caught up in this. At this time, I must stress that we have no reason to believe that the teacher was involved in any way, but we must check every possible reason as to why this innocent girl was taken."

***

Samantha handed back the paper to Jessica and stood with tears in her eyes, and she could tell that Jessica was trying to hold back the tears as well. After a few minutes they succeeded, but Samantha stood quietly for another minute or so whilst wondering about something that her mother had said at the campsite. She couldn't remember why it seemed familiar.

Jessica looked at Samantha. It seemed that she had forgotten about the mysterious man that had dropped the piece of paper about the Quiz Challenge. "It seems you have forgotten what your mother said about the Quiz Challenge." Jessica sighed. "She said that the building where the school is now has the trophies hidden somewhere. I think that man who dropped the piece of paper when we went to collect Laura from the school is the teacher who is missing."

Samantha's jaw almost dropped. "I forgot about that." Samantha sighed. "Maybe we should tell someone about this." She was scared someone would come and try to find the trophies.

"I think we should try to find the trophies first; otherwise, I doubt anyone will believe us." Jessica sighed. "You know what grownups are like."

"Yeah, okay, that is what we will do." Samantha giggled. She wasn't sure if she agreed with Jessica about the grownups not believing them, but she would do what Jessica wanted. "I think we might need to tell a couple of people we trust to keep a secret. How about Ben and that girl we talked to in the cloakroom, Olivia?" She looked at Jessica, wondering what her friend was thinking.

"I agree we need to tell someone else, or we could be looking for ages. So you think Ben and Olivia, then I'll go along with that." Jessica smiled. She wasn't sure about Olivia, but she knew that Samantha would have wanted to tell the teachers, so she would trust Samantha's judgement on the new girl. "We can tell Olivia tonight if you want, and we can tell Ben when we see him. He'll be over at the boys' dorms, so we can't go to him now," Jessica said truthfully.

Samantha looked at Jessica. She was sure that Jessica would have argued about telling the other two and was surprised when she had agreed to tell Olivia and Ben. She was glad that Jessica had agreed that they needed more people to look through the building to find clues about the fire and the trophy the brothers stole. "I'll agree to that." Samantha smiled. She wasn't going to argue with Jessica, even though she wanted to find them and tell them everything now, but she would wait. She had to admit if they told Olivia when everyone else was asleep, there wasn't that much of a chance that they could be overheard.

Jessica was about to reply when suddenly Mrs. Baker walked up to them. "Hello, Jessica. Did you have a good holiday?"

"I did, thank you, Mrs. Baker," Jessica replied. "It was odd walking past where the school used to be. I went past it a couple of times. It seems the man wanted it back so a friend could change it into a shop."

"Well, I think the school will be happy here. It seems like a lovely place, and there is the campsite not far from the village, which reminds me—but don't tell anyone else yet, I got permission to tell Samantha, and since you're here, Jessica, I'll tell you—the school will be having a camping trip once a year in the summer. We don't know what week yet, but anyone who goes to the school can come as long as he or she has his or her parents' permission."

"That is cool." Samantha smiled at her mother. She loved the camping trip this term, though she didn't like getting into trouble for swimming across the lake to see if the house was haunted.

Mrs. Baker looked at her daughter and Jessica and then remembered why she had come out in the first place. "I came to tell you both that everyone has to be in the hall at 5:10 p.m." Mrs. Baker looked at her watch. "I must be going now," and with that she left them and headed back to the school.

Samantha watched her mother leave and then looked at her watch. "So we have a few hours to spare." Samantha sighed; she was going to get bored before then.

"Don't worry. It'll soon pass." Jessica giggled.

They looked around for a bit and then headed back inside. At four, they decided they'd welcome the two busses that were bringing the children from the station at the town fifteen miles away. The time flew by after that, and soon they had listened to Miss Moore telling them the rules, then they all talked until 9:00 p.m., when they had to go to bed.

Chapter 12

First Prank

At midnight, Jessica snuck up to Samantha's bed and poked her, hoping her friend wouldn't make too much noise.

"What the—" Samantha said through a yawn. She was only half awake when she realised it was Jessica who had woken her up. "This had best be important." Samantha yawned as she sat up.

"It is." Jessica laughed, though she was trying to keep the noise down so she didn't wake any of the other girls.

"Oh, yeah, have you woken Olivia up yet?" Samantha didn't want to move. "Because if you haven't, you can do it now." Samantha smiled evilly. "It's your turn to do it."

Jessica poked her friend in the chest and smiled. "Yeah, and since we probably won't do it again, you won't have to do it."

"Nope." She giggled. "That's why I said you can do it. I don't know if she'd eat me alive for waking her up at this time."

"True." Then looking at her friend's face, Jessica smiled. "Okay then, I'll do it this time, though next time you can do it."

Jessica left Samantha and came back a few minutes later with Olivia, who looked just as bad as Samantha. They both weren't night people by the looks of things. Olivia sat down on the edge of the bed as Samantha sat up to make room for them both.

"What's going on?" Olivia asked. She was very confused and wanted to get to bed.

"Shhh," Jessica whispered. "We don't want to wake everyone else up." She poked her head out of the curtains around Samantha's bed to make sure no one else was awake.

"Oh, sorry." Olivia blushed. She had forgotten they could get into trouble if they were caught out of bed at this time of the night. She whispered, "What's so important that you got me out of bed?"

Samantha looked at Olivia. "Well, we can see you're going to be a good friend to us, and so we have decided we can trust you to help us with something very important." Samantha smiled; she had a good feeling about that.

For the next ten minutes, Olivia listened to everything that Samantha and Jessica told her. The only problem was that they hadn't realised that Natasha was awake and listening, too. She had already decided that she would find the trophy with the help of her friends Emily and Richard before Samantha did. She had only woken up toward the end, so she hadn't heard about Laura going missing; otherwise, she might not have promised herself to do everything in her tracks to stop Samantha from finding the trophies. By the time they had finished telling Olivia and she had promised not to tell anyone else, Natasha had fallen asleep.

When Jessica went back to her bed, she checked to make sure everyone was asleep. She knew how important it was for people not to know what they were up to. Jessica was soon asleep, but it took Olivia a bit longer. She was glad that Jessica and Samantha trusted her and was sure they were going to be good friends, but she had this feeling that they didn't know what they were getting into and was sure it would be better if they told a teacher, even if it was Samantha's mother or father. Even though Olivia wanted to tell a teacher, she wouldn't, because she had promised she wouldn't, and she never broke a promise.

The next day's lesson meant that they couldn't tell Ben anything until the day students had gone home, so at 5:00 p.m. they finally were able to sit down with Ben and tell him everything that they had told Olivia the night before. Meanwhile, Natasha was telling her two friends what she had overheard and what they were going to do to stop Samantha from finding the trophies first, though there was a problem, as Natasha's friends wanted to tell the teachers and get Samantha and her gang into trouble for not saying anything, but Natasha wanted to keep the trophies for herself. Her friends had no idea why and were a bit scared of being told off if they were caught with the trophy, but in the end, Natasha convinced them to do it, and so they sat for the next ten minutes deciding what the first prank would be.

***

For the past week, nothing much had happened. The students had been too busy with work, so it wasn't until Saturday when the students had the day off that the fun started. The day started out bright and sunny and there was nothing peculiar about that morning to suggest anything bad was about to happen.

The first thing to go wrong was when Olivia went out to have a bath. She was one of the first to have one that day, but when she opened the door, a bucketful of water hit her, and she screamed the place down. It was only 7:00 a.m., and as it was Saturday, the students normally would have had a lie-in, but because even the boys heard Olivia scream at the other end of the school, Miss Moore decided the best thing to do would be to get the cooks started with the breakfasts. She was glad that they hadn't complained about having to get breakfast ready early. On the weekend, breakfast was served at 9:00 a.m., so Miss Moore made it clear this was a one-off.

"Once you have finished your breakfast, please stay in the building until 10:00 a.m. According to Mr. Baker, the juniors are still asleep in their building." Miss Moore smiled. "Breakfast should be ready soon."

They didn't have to wait long for breakfast, and it took about five minutes for everyone to be served. A half an hour later they had finished breakfast and been sent to make sure that everything was tidy with their dorm rooms. After that, they gathered in their common room until the bell rang at 10:20 a.m. for them to go for a walk. Samantha knew this would be the best time to talk to Olivia, Jessica, and Ben without the chance to be overheard, and so she went to speak with her mother, who was on duty that weekend. She knocked on the classroom door and waited until her mother said enter.

"Hello, Samantha." Mrs Baker smiled. "What can I do for you?"

"I was wondering if you would take me, Jessica, Olivia, and Ben for a walk, instead of going with the group. I want you to meet my friends," Samantha lied. She wasn't going to tell her mother the real reason.

"That sounds like a great idea." Mrs Baker smiled. She hadn't spent much time with Samantha and thought it was a great idea for her to get to know Samantha's friends. "I'd love to, and I'm sure Miss Moore won't mind."

Samantha smiled at her mother. "Thank you for agreeing. I hope we can." Samantha then left the room to find the others whilst her mother went to Miss Moore to see if it was okay. When Samantha came back with her friends, her mother was already back from the head's office.

"Miss Moore was going to suggest going out in little groups, so it's okay for me to take you lot for a walk." Mrs Baker smiled. "Though your father can't come, Samantha. The juniors are staying together in the school. Only the seniors are allowed out today, and next week it will be the juniors' turn. Oh, and before I forget, I checked to see if you all have signed forms to leave the school grounds, and you all have."

"Yeah, I checked before asking you. I think it's a great idea, and it's only fair, that if we go for a walk this time that the juniors are allowed to go for a walk next week."

"I agree." Olivia smiled. She had become good friends with Samantha and nine times out of ten would agree with what Samantha said.

So it was at 10:45 a.m. that Mrs. Baker and her small group left. They were going to have lunch in the village and then have a walk before heading back to school. Mrs. Baker promised Miss Moore that she would look after them and that they would stay away from the lake.

"Mrs. Baker, where are we going first?" Jessica asked. She was curious. She'd been on loads of walks with Mr. and Mrs. Baker when she and Samantha had been at Manchester together, and she knew it was going to be fun.

"I was thinking we could go and see what the village is like," Mrs. Baker replied. She smiled at her small group as they left the school grounds.

"That sounds cool." All the others smiled. They had all wanted to see the village since coming for the camping trip in the summer.

***

They hadn't seen that Natasha and Emily were following them. Unfortunately for Natasha, Richard wasn't well, so he had been told to stay in his bed by Miss Moore.

"Natasha, I can't go any further." Emily sighed. "I don't have permission to leave the school grounds, and if I am caught outside of them, I'll be in trouble. I promised my parents I wouldn't get into any trouble."

"We won't get caught," Natasha said. "Did I get caught at the last school we went to when I snuck out?"

"No, but it was close on a few occasions," Emily said as she looked around anxiously. She was hoping that she could talk Natasha out of sneaking out of the school. "Why don't we just stay here and look around the school?"

"Because we'll never find out what Samantha and her friends are planning that way. They still haven't even started to look for the trophies." Natasha shot a piercing look at Emily. "Now, come on, coward." With that being said, she left the school yard to follow Samantha, making sure she couldn't be seen.

Emily looked scared and confused. She wanted to go with her friend but didn't want any trouble. It wasn't until Natasha called her a coward that Emily followed her. She hated being called a coward and was going to prove that she wasn't.

***

For the next hour, nothing much happened. It wasn't until they went for dinner that the fun started. Olivia had a strange feeling, but she waited until Mrs. Baker had gone to pay for dinner before she told the others.

"Did you lot have this strange feeling we were being followed?" Olivia asked.

"Yeah, but I just thought it was my imagination," Jessica replied. "I'm sure it's just because we were in a strange place."

"I agree." Ben hated the fact he was the only boy here, but he found it fun spending time with Samantha and the others and wanted to help Samantha get her friend back.

"Anyway, whilst my mother is away, let's talk about what we are going to do." Samantha got out a pen and notepad from her pocket.

Meanwhile, Natasha and Emily had ordered drinks and sat down at the table near the others where they couldn't be seen. Unbeknownst to all the students was that two men also were nearby trying to figure out how to get into Moore Field School, and when they heard Samantha and her gang talking about the school, they couldn't help but listen.

Mrs. Baker came back and was shocked to see Miss Robins running into the shop. "There you are, Mrs. Baker." She smiled. "I've come to see if you have taken Natasha and Emily with you. A junior boy saw them leaving just after you."

As soon as Miss Robins came in, Natasha and Emily left. They knew if they were caught in the café, they would have a lot of explaining to do.

"No, I don't have them," Mrs. Baker said. "I have no idea where they are." She looked at the children and gave them the food and drinks she had ordered. "Miss Robins, can you stay here with my group, then take them back to school? You can even have my coffee."

"Okay, Mrs. Baker. I'll take good care of them." Miss Robins smiled. Miss Moore had warned her that Mrs. Baker would want to look for the two missing girls.

Mrs. Baker left the café straight after that, and Miss Robins sat down with the children. She was glad that she didn't have to look for the two missing students because she wouldn't know where to start. After twenty minutes, the students had eaten their lunch.

"I'm sorry you won't get to do what you planned to do this afternoon, but we must return to school." Miss Robins finished the last of her coffee and smiled at the students.

"It's okay." Ben smiled. "I know it is important for you to find the missing students." Ben and Olivia stood up and took the plates and cups to the counter.

It took thirty minutes to walk back to the school, and when they got there, they saw that Mrs. Baker was talking with Miss Moore. The women were confused, as they had found Emily and Natasha near the front gate but on the school site. The young junior was sure they had left the school grounds, but without proof, the school staff couldn't do anything.

Chapter 13

Two Plans Are Decided On

A few days after the incident, everything was starting to settle down. Miss Moore was certain that the two students had been out of the school grounds, but without any proof, they couldn't do anything but warn the girls that if they were caught out off the school grounds, they would be in serious trouble. Natasha and Emily were both glad they hadn't been caught—twice they had just got back onto the grounds when Miss Moore found them. Their excuse for being near the gate wasn't good, and that was why Miss Moore was sure they had been out of the school. Mrs. Baker had almost caught them outside the coffee shop, but they had managed to hide before she had seen them.

The following Thursday things started getting weird again. The school had finished lessons and Samantha, Ben, Olivia, and Jessica were sitting outside on the grass. The sun was shining brightly and there wasn't a single cloud in the sky. Many other students were out and about making the most of the beautiful weather. Jessica had spotted two men whom she recognised and a third she didn't know, and she had been watching them from the corner of her eyes for about ten minutes. She was about to mention them when one of their classmates, Harry, suddenly came running up.

"Samantha, I just thought I'd warn you about this man snooping outside the gate. He's looking in your direction." Harry had no idea if they had seen the men, so he made sure they knew they were being watching.

Jessica looked at Harry and smiled. "I've seen them, and I'm sure they won't do anything. Just forget about them. Anyway, they are off now, and I'm sure Samantha will tell her mother," Jessica said as she pointed at the men, who were just leaving. Whilst the others weren't looking, she nudged Samantha and gave her a wink.

"Yeah, I can do that." Samantha realised that Jessica wanted to speak to her with the others without Harry being here. She looked at Harry and smiled. "I'm glad that you told us, and I'll tell my mother about the men."

"That is good." Harry then remembered that he was meeting a friend, and so he ran off back toward the school whilst Samantha, Olivia, and Ben looked at Jessica.

Jessica decided that she should tell them about the guys that Harry had seen. "The guys Harry saw were the same ones Samantha and I saw at the school in Manchester when we went to meet Laura that day, the teacher and the older man. There was a third man I don't know, so I would have to say that Laura must be somewhere around here, though it could take us ages to find her." Jessica sighed.

"We'll do it." Olivia smiled. "With me and Ben helping you, we will be at an advantage, because even though they have seen us talking, they don't know that we know about the treasure that is supposed to be hidden here."

Samantha told them, "I want you two to promise that if anything happens to me and Jessica, you will go and find my mother and Miss Moore and tell them everything." Samantha put on her most serious face. "I don't want you to try anything stupid."

Olivia and Ben knew that, when Samantha was serious, it was best to do what she said. "Okay." They knew it was the right thing to do.

"Now that we have that sorted out, I think we should get off. It's now 12:55, and lessons will be starting soon. Those who left for dinner are now coming back." Samantha pointed to the students coming through the front gate.

The others looked and, sure enough, the day students were returning for afternoon classes. It was amazing how fast time flew when you were with mates, and Olivia was wishing it didn't. Truth be told, she hadn't fitted in at the main school in the town ten miles away from Lakeview, so when Miss Moore had brought her school here, her father had decided this could be a fresh start for her. Her dad was in the Navy, and her mother had died when she was younger, which is why she was a boarder. She would stay with her aunt in Leeds on holidays unless her dad was home. She hadn't told the others about her life but would tell them if the time came. She was suddenly brought back to reality by Samantha, who was nudging her. Samantha had realised that Olivia hadn't moved when the others had set off and had come back to see if she was okay. "Come on, slow coach." Samantha giggled. "It's seemed like you were miles away then."

"Sorry, I was thinking about something." Olivia smiled back, though the faraway look in Olivia's eyes hadn't escaped Samantha.

"Are you alright?" Samantha asked.

"I'm fine." Olivia looked at Samantha. She had no idea why Samantha would ask such a question. Did she look upset, or did Samantha just have a feeling something was going on? "I think we should go and catch up to the others, or they will think something is up." Olivia raced off toward the school.

Samantha looked at Olivia as she ran off. She was a bit upset that Olivia hadn't told her what was wrong. She was sure something was bothering Olivia and promised herself that she would find out. What Samantha didn't know as she ran after Olivia was that something was about to happen that would put this at the back of her mind.

***

The men who had been at the school gates went into the building where they were keeping Laura, and Mr. Walker gave her some food. She was guarded by a man who never left the room, which was a decent size. It was covered in newspapers, one—just a day old—saying that the police had reason to believe that Walker might be involved. All the others had said he might have been taken, as well, though one had said that some evidence had come up that shocked the school and the police: Even though the man's background had been checked and he had glowing references, he had, in fact, a criminal record and falsified documents from a school that didn't exist. The question was, why hadn't this been checked? That day's paper had a picture of the head of the school in Manchester and famous people calling for her to stand down. Prime Minister Tim Simpson announced that the Education Department would be looking into the failings to make sure nothing like this ever happened again.

"Don't worry, Laura. Once we have everything we need, we will let you go." Walker smiled as he put the food on the table. "I brought you some food." Truth be told, he was starting to like Laura and was sad that she had been dragged into it, but they needed her to get Samantha and Jessica to cooperate. At the moment, that was difficult because they never left school without a teacher present.

"Why don't I believe you?" Laura looked straight into his eyes, trying to find any hint of weakness.

Walker left the room then. He was really upset that Laura didn't believe him, though he knew it would be hard to convince her. The old man looked up as his friend came into the room, his hand clenched into a ball. He thumped the table, making the others jump. What had started out as a three-man job now had five men, and so there were another two in the room.

"We can't wait any longer," the old man said. "We're going to have to go into the school and try to find some clues. I'm sure Miss Moore knows something, so the best place to search would be her office."

"Well, what do you want us to do, go in tonight and search her office?" Walker joked.

"That isn't a bad idea." The old man smiled at his friend. They had been working together for ages. "We need to get this done. There are a few bigger things we could be doing. Someone phoned me and offered us some work. Apparently, the Navy is bringing in a new machine that will sell for millions, and we get a split if we're involved. They want us to take the man—funny enough, his daughter goes to a school around here—and that means we need to get this treasure found within the next few weeks."

"Okay." He had only been joking, but if they had another job lined up, they would have to get the treasure out soon or leave it and then figure out a way to get the treasure from anyone else who might find it.

"Okay, so take those two with you," the old man said as he indicated the other men. "And try not to make too much noise. I'm sure everyone should be in bed around 11:00 p.m., so if you go after then, you should be able to search Miss Moore's office without the school being up."

***

What the old man didn't know was that Natasha and Emily had decided that they would put their plan into action that night too. Thomas, who had agreed to help Natasha, had decided he couldn't go through with it and had begged Emily not to be involved because he didn't want her get into trouble. Even though Emily knew she would be in big trouble, she owed Natasha for all the times she had helped Emily at their last school. Richard had agreed to be their lookout.

***

For the next few hours, everything was quiet. At six o'clock that evening, the old man was at the table at the old house with the others, sitting there with a frown on his face. They had a few hours before he sent in a few people to try to find out if the headmistress knew about the treasure, and they hadn't even thought of a plan, which normally they would have done the day before.

"We need to think of something," the old man said as he slammed his hand on the table, causing everyone who was around the table to jump.

"Well, if we go in just before midnight, everyone will be asleep. We can locate the head's office as quickly and quietly as we can. That should give us a couple of hours to find anything. If we don't find anything, then I don't think the headmistress knew this place was where the brothers hid the treasure," John said. He and Walker were the two who were going into the school.

"I don't agree with that." Walker laughed as he finished off the cigarette he had been smoking. "I can't think of any other reason why she would bring the school here. She knew about the theft that occurred after Moore Field School had won the competition, and as the captain, she would be keen to put the trophies back where they belong. How they managed to get all the trophies from every school without being seen is beyond me."

"I've been trying to figure that out too." The old man nodded his head in agreement. "The only thing I can think of was they hit every school with the help of some friends." The old man knew that was improbable, but it was the only way he could see them getting the trophies without being caught. "Okay, I agree with your plan." He didn't want to spend all night thinking of plans.

Chapter 14

A Shocking Discovery

It was 11:00 p.m. when Natasha and Emily left their bedroom to meet Richard near the head's room. They were just about to talk when Samantha, Jessica, and Olivia came down the stairs to find the treasure to give to the men in exchange for Laura. They were sure the men had her. When they got downstairs, they were surprised to see the others.

"What are you doing here?" Samantha asked. Before anyone else could speak, a voice behind them made them all jump.

"How many of us are involved in this?" Ben asked, as he joined the others. He was confused to how Natasha, Emily, and Richard had found out.

"Just the ones you know about, Ben," Jessica replied, looking straight at Natasha, wondering if she would explain what they were doing out of bed.

"We were just—" Emily started, but before she could finish, Natasha was butting in.

"What are you doing up?" she asked. "You can't say anything to us when you are up, as well." Natasha folded her arms. She wasn't going to tell them unless they told her what they were doing up. "Why are you up?"

"We were setting up a prank," Ben lied. He didn't think they would fall for it, but he thought it was worth a try. "And before you ask, you can't help. We all have a part, and we don't want to disrupt them this late," he added when he realised that Emily was about to speak.

Emily looked at Ben and smiled. "Well, we were about to play a trick on a teacher," Emily lied. She had decided that if Ben didn't want to tell them, then why should she tell what they were doing?

Samantha, realising that no one was going to give way, decided she would have to trust the others. "I think we should tell them," she said as she looked at the clock. They had been talking for five minutes, and she was surprised that no one had come to see what was going on.

"Are you sure?" Olivia was surprised. She wasn't sure if they should trust the others, and she didn't want them to find the treasure and run off.

"I am," Samantha lied. She wasn't sure, but they couldn't stand talking here for ages, and so for the next twenty minutes, they all listened whilst Samantha spoke.

Once Samantha had finished, Natasha spoke up. "I knew about the treasure. I overheard you lot talking, but I didn't know about Laura." Natasha sighed. "We'll help you." She didn't like helping people, but if the treasure would help get this girl Laura free, then she would, for once, like to say she helped. Once this was over, though, she was going back to doing things for herself.

"Thanks." Samantha smiled. She looked at the others, who were just as shocked as she was. They had all thought that Natasha was spoilt and wouldn't do anything for anyone but herself. She was about to say something else when she saw the look on Olivia's face; it looked like she was thinking hard about something. Samantha wanted to ask her what was wrong, but she decided she would talk to her later.

Samantha, Olivia, and Jessica went to look in the basement, whilst the others went to see what they could find out in the school library. They had decided that there might be some information in a book. They knew it was a longshot, but they thought that it was one worth taking. They looked for half an hour before coming back to where they had left. Samantha and her group were the last to arrive.

"Did you find anything?" Samantha asked.

"Nothing. You?" Ben replied. He had thought he had found something in the library, but it turned out to be nothing.

"We couldn't find anything." Samantha sighed. She had a look in her eyes that made everyone shiver.

"What are you planning?" Jessica didn't like the look in her friend's eyes.

"I was thinking there is one place that we haven't been to, though if we are caught there, we will be in trouble," Samantha replied truthfully.

Ben and Richard had realised what Samantha was talking about. "I'm not going in there," they both said at the same time. "No way am I going in the head's office."

Jessica and Olivia looked shocked, and then they too starting shaking their heads. They weren't going into the head's office for anyone.

Samantha was about to argue back when suddenly there was a bang, and they hurried off to find out where it was coming from.

***

"Quiet." Walker looked at the man who had made the noise. "Now all we have to do is find the head's office."

"Walker," the other man said, "I think we are in it." He took a sign off the table that said "Miss Moore."

"Don't—" Walker looked angry, then his face changed to a surprised expression. "I think you might be right. What a bit of luck." He laughed. "Come on, let's have a look through the office before someone comes."

***

Samantha had sent Olivia to get her mother whilst they went to find out where the noise was coming from. They had decided that getting into trouble was better than letting someone destroy the school, because they had no idea who was at the school or what their intention was.

"I think it's coming from in there," Emily whispered. Up until this point, she had been too scared to say anything.

Samantha was about to open the door when Natasha stopped her by tugging her arm away.

"What are you doing?" Samantha shouted angrily.

"Look whose door it is," Natasha said, keeping calm, though she herself was angry because the men inside the room had just probably heard Samantha screaming. If they came in through that window, they would probably be long gone now.

Samantha looked at Natasha and sighed. "I'm sorry about shouting at you." She couldn't believe she had shouted, because it would probably mean whoever was inside the room would have escape; then Natasha spoke again, and Samantha looked at the sign. "I wonder what they wanted with Miss Moore's office."

"I do—" Ben started but then looked up into the sky. There were three ghosts standing there. "What the—"

"Please don't run or shout," the ghost on the left said. They were wearing 1950s clothes and looked like they had died young, perhaps school-age, Samantha thought, judging by their appearance.

"We aren't going to." Samantha smiled at the ghost. She was about to ask something when there was a scream from behind. The students turned round to see Olivia screaming, with Mrs. Baker trying to quiet her. It took Olivia a couple of seconds to stop.

"We want to know why Miss Moore went back on her word." The ghost in the middle did a loop-the-loop in the air and then stopped just short of Mrs. Baker.

Before anything else could be said, Miss Moore came to see what was going on. She was annoyed when she saw that the ghosts had come out of the basement and was about to ask them why when she heard them say she had broken her promise.

"Have any of you been in the basement?" Miss Moore asked the girls. She knew Mrs. Baker wouldn't have, but she had forgotten to tell the students that the basement was out of bounds. She would do that tomorrow.

"We're sorry, Miss Moore. We didn't know we weren't allowed," Samantha said truthfully. She didn't want to tell Miss Moore yet, in case they could solve the problem on their own.

"I'll tell the school tomorrow. I forgot at the start of the term," Miss Moore said and then looked at the ghosts. "I'm sorry, it won't happen again."

"Well, I'm glad." The ghosts smiled at Miss Moore and then bowed to her. Before the students could speak, the ghosts had floated off back down the corridors toward where the basement was.

"What was—" Olivia started to say, but Miss Moore cut across her.

"It was nothing. They were just ghosts that have been here for ages, and when I bought the building, I promised I wouldn't disturb them." Miss Moore smiled. "Now I believe you should all be in bed."

"Yeah, it's late," Mrs. Baker agreed with Miss Moore. "I'll see them off to bed."

Back in the girls' room, Natasha, Emily, Olivia, Jessica, and Samantha were talking about what had happened that night.

"I wonder why Miss Moore promised them no one would go in the basement." Jessica sighed.

"What has all this to do with Laura?" Samantha wondered. She was really confused about that.

"I have a feeling that—" Jessica started but then stopped as she heard some banging on the front door and Miss Moore shrieking.

"I wonder what's going on," Olivia asked. They wanted to get up but didn't, in case Miss Moore told them off.

"We'd best get to sleep," Natasha said. Before she could say anything else, a smiling Miss Moore came into the room.

"Girls, I have some good news! Laura has been found. That was the police, and they wanted to know if we had somewhere she could stay for the night. Her parents are coming tomorrow to speak to me about transferring her here." She looked at Jessica and Samantha. "Isn't that good news?"

"Yes, it is." Samantha smiled. "Where is she now?"

"I thought it was best she slept on her own, so we gave her your mother's room. Your mother is going to drive home and sleep there for the night." Miss Moore then put on a stern face. "Anyway, unless you all want detention for a month, you will all go to your own beds." She had just realised they were all around Samantha's bed.

The girls knew that when Miss Moore had that face on, they had to do what they were told, so they all scurried off to their beds.

Miss Moore waited until they were all safely in their beds before leaving the room. She was sure they were hiding something and made a note to keep an eye on them.

***

Meanwhile, in the building where they were keeping Laura, John and Walker came back to something unexpected. The man who had been guarding Laura was unconscious, and Laura was gone. The scream that came out of the old man's mouth when he came downstairs was ear piercing.

"What happened?" he yelled. He had been asleep for a few hours and this had happened. He was glad that John was back because if he wasn't, then they were in trouble.

"She said she needed the loo, and when I untied her, she kicked me and then hit me with something," the man said truthfully. "I'm sorry."

"Well, she could be anywhere now, so we had better leave before the police come. I'll give you five minutes to get everything ready." The old man snapped at everyone. He wasn't in the best mood, and within twenty minutes, the house they had been in had been completely emptied. Nothing was left, and they knew that they would have to come back to

Moore Field School. By then, he hoped everyone would have forgotten them. What they didn't realise was that their new mission from their master was connected to this mission, but as they say, that is another story.

Lightning Source UK Ltd.
Milton Keynes UK
UKOW04f2255220215

246654UK00002B/27/P